RESISTING THE
MOON

NEW YORK TIMES AND USA TODAY BESTSELLING AUTHOR

L.P. DOVER

L.P. Dover
Copyright © by L.P. Dover
Edited by: Victoria Schmitz | Crimson Tide Editorial
Cover designed by: RBA Designs

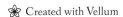 Created with Vellum

INTRODUCTION

After writing a gazillion books by this point, my list of acknowledgments have grown. It'd take me a whole novel length book to thank each and every one of you who have helped me on my journey. With that being said, I want to send a big THANK YOU to everyone out there! Without you, my worlds wouldn't be able to exist.

PROLOGUE

TYLA

Thirty Years Ago

"**A**re you sure this is what you want?" my mother asked. For the past few months, she had asked me the same question repeatedly. You'd think she'd get the point; my answer wasn't going to change. Looking into her gray gaze, I smiled.

"Yes, it's what I want," I said, ruffling her curly blonde hair. She may have been a hundred years older than me, but we looked about the same age. I was twenty-three years old in human years, but it was nice to know I could live to be five hundred and only have the appearance of a forty-year-old.

I'd gotten my looks and stubbornness from my mother, and my fighting skills from my father. He was thrilled Finn and I were going to lead the pack together, but my mother didn't share in his enthusiasm.

Finn Olcan was our alpha, and currently standing just across the room, watching us. I guess you could say we were having a party for our future union. In one week, we'd be mated and living happily ever after. That was what I kept telling myself as least.

Grasping my elbow, my mom leaned in close, her voice a soft whisper. "He's not your true mate, sweetheart. You need to give it more time."

I sighed in defeat. "That's something I don't have and you know it."

"I know, but this isn't the life I wanted for you. I want you to find your true mate, like your father and I did. You won't ever be fully happy with Finn, nor he with you."

"It's better than being dead," I snapped.

Or worse, it could mean the lives of my family. If Finn and I didn't mate by the next full moon, I'd have a fight on my hands. Not to mention, it'd be a war amongst our kind.

Vincent Connery, alpha of the Sierra Pack, wanted a strong female to be his mate. It was rumored he'd killed his last two after they gave birth to his children. Unfortunately, no one knew the absolute truth. I, for one, didn't want to get close enough to him to find out. What made it even more disgusting was that he had a son the same age as me. Mating with Finn was the only way to keep me safe, as well as making sure our pack was strong.

Finn was a good-looking man and someone I was very much attracted to, but the magic of true mates never came for us. We'd taken each other's blood the night before, hoping we'd be able to hear each other's thoughts. Unfortunately, it never happened; therefore, disappointing us even further. I cared for him deeply, but I didn't know what else to do.

My mother squeezed my arm. "Here he comes, my dear. I'll give you some privacy."

Finn acknowledged my mother with a nod and a smile. "Sophia," he said warmly.

She nodded back. "Finn."

Taking my hand, he led me outside and pressed me against the side of my parents' house, our bodies hidden by a set of bushes. "I love you, Tyla. I know you're not happy about last night, but there's still time. We don't need magic to tell us we're meant to be mated."

"No, but it'd help. I care about you Finn, and I do love you. I just wish it'd happen for us." The only truly mated couples in our pack were my parents, and my aunt and uncle, Sarah and Benjamin. My parents were also the oldest. Everyone looked up to them, yet resented them for being complete. To find your true mate was rare, but we kept praying for a time the magic would come back to us.

Sighing, he leaned down and kissed me, placing his forehead to mine. "Stay with me tonight," he murmured.

I sucked in a nervous breath. "You mean—"

"Yes, baby, all night."

Was I ready for that? We'd messed around for the past couple of years, but we'd always ended it before we got too far. The thought excited and terrified me all at once. I had never slept with a man before.

His hands slid from my neck, down to my breasts; his arousal pressing into my leg. My heart thundered in my chest. He could hear it and a smile splayed across his face.

"Sounds like you're just as excited as I am," he murmured low, kissing his way across my collarbone.

Giving in, I tilted my neck to the side. "Just go slow with me, Finn. That's all I ask."

"Tyla, wake up!" Finn shouted. At first, I thought I was dreaming, but when I opened my eyes, I was naked in his bed, my pulse spiking the moment I spotted him. Ripping the blankets off, he helped me out of bed, pulling me into his arms.

"What's going on?" The look on his face terrified me.

"Vincent's wolves are closing in. They were spotted about fifteen miles out. I need to get you away from here." He grabbed my clothes off the floor. "Put these on."

"I want to stay and fight," I said, tossing the clothes onto the bed.

Eyes glowing, he growled. "If something happens to me, Vincent will lay claim to you. I need you gone. As soon as it's over, I'll come for you." A loud knock sounded on the

door downstairs. "*Please*, Tyla. I need you to do this for me."
He kissed me hard and raced out of the room. I threw on my
clothes and cringed when I heard my parents' voices down
below.

I raced downstairs and my mother's look of disappointment was evident by the scowl on her face. My father and
Finn were already outside talking strategies. "We have to
go," she demanded. Grabbing my hand, my mother pulled
me outside to their waiting car. The guys were standing by
the passenger door, and it was filled with luggage and boxes.

"What the hell's going on? Why aren't we shifting?" I
asked.

Finn clasped my face in his strong hands. "I had them
be prepared, in case something like this happened. I had a
feeling Vincent would come for you. He's done the same
thing before with another pack."

"And what happened to them?"

He huffed and held me tighter. "He wiped them out.
But I'm not going to let that happen here. Now go."

"Oh my God," I gasped.

"Tyla, let's go," my father urged.

Finn kissed me one last time and stepped back when
howling echoed through the trees. "Go," he commanded.
"I'll be with you soon." He ripped off his clothes and
shifted, racing into the trees. The enemy pack drew closer
and I could hear their snarls.

"Tyla!" my father shouted.

Turning on my heel, I ran to the car and jumped into
the backseat. We took off out of the driveway, tires spinning
on the gravel. We were in the middle of nowhere. If we
didn't get out of the woods, the wolves would catch us.

"We're never going to get away from them," I shouted.

My father pressed the gas and my body jerked back. "We will. We just need to get to the main road." The night was foggy and dark, leaving everything bathed in an ominous glow from the moonlight.

The hair on the back of my neck stood on end, my pulse racing. Then, I saw a set of glowing eyes in the distance. But they weren't alone. "They're here," I growled.

After that, everything moved in slow motion. More eyes appeared and what sounded like a thunderous gunshot rang out.

"Hold on," my father shouted. He lost control of the car and we went sailing down a ravine. I was jarred forward as we slammed into a tree; the car, nothing but a smoking pile of junk. My father kicked his door open and ripped mine off its hinges so I could get out. He rushed over to the other side of the car to help my mother, who had blood streaming down her face from a gash above her eye.

"Mom, are you okay?" I gasped, running over to her.

She hissed in pain when my father touched the wound. "I'll be fine. We need to shift." Growls erupted all around us; they were close. I could hear fighting from a distance, the smell of blood permeating the air.

"You wanna fight?" I shouted. Ripping off my clothes, I stared the wolves down before shifting. *Come and get me.*

ONE

"Can you believe the turn out?" Bailey shouted over the din of the bar. She was my friend, a royal, alpha female and the mate of our pack leader, Ryker Whitemore. She practically glowed with her whitish-blonde hair and bright blue eyes.

"Of course everyone would be here. How could they pass up the chance to celebrate the little one?" Once news spread about their pregnancy, the party was set up the very next day. I looked around; the bar was filled with nothing but wolves.

Smiling, Bailey turned her gaze to the crowd. "I can honestly say that everything seems to be right for the first time in my life." I wished I felt like that.

My focus landed on her younger sister, Faith, who threw her head back and laughed at something Cedric said. She was beautiful, just like Bailey, with the classic whitish-blonde hair of the Arctic wolf. Surely Cedric wasn't *that* funny. He was Ryker's second-in-command and a complete pain in my ass. I loved him though, even if he did always find ways to get on my nerves.

Then there was Colin, Bailey's older brother and a Royal Arctic wolf who couldn't seem to take his crystal blue eyes off of me. I tried ignoring him, but it was hard when I could feel his power across the room. We seriously needed to get rid of all the testosterone. Having five alphas in one pack was insanity.

"Tyla? You still in there?" Bailey laughed.

Clearing my throat, I pulled her into a hug. "Sorry about that. I am truly happy for you, Bailey. You deserve all of this and more."

She stepped back and smiled at something over my shoulder. "So do you," she replied with a wink. When she turned to leave, I felt him, the man I didn't want to want. Who was I kidding? All of the royal males in our pack had an advantage and I didn't like it. Their power could draw you in like an addict, salivating over your next fix. It sucked donkey ass.

"Can I help you?" I asked, turning to face Sebastian Lyall.

His whitish-blond hair was perfectly coifed in messy spikes, his light blue, button down shirt matching the color of his eyes. The last thing I needed was to look into them. He'd had me tongue tied several times in the past and it ended up making me look like an idiot.

Smirking, Sebastian stepped closer, holding out a hand. "Would you care to dance?"

Rolling my eyes, I nodded toward the group of women in the corner who watched his every move. "Why don't you ask one of your groupies? I'm sure they'd be more than willing."

He and his brothers, Micah and Zayne, along with Colin, were hot commodities in our pack. They were all royal wolves—the elite. No female could resist them, except me that is. I couldn't complain though; the royals helped make our pack invincible.

Sebastian leaned closer, his gaze serious. "I asked *you*, Tyla Rand. Besides, there's something I need to tell you."

"Why do we have to dance in order for you to spill? Just say it now."

Chuckling, he grabbed my hand and pulled me to the dance floor. "What's the matter, afraid to be close to me? I promise I won't bite."

Right. Huffing, I reluctantly walked onto the dance floor just when the tempo changed to a slower, sensual beat. "You've got to be kidding me," I growled. Other couples joined in and held each other, swaying to the music, while I stood there like a fool.

Grabbing my other hand, Sebastian pulled my arms around his shoulders and put his around my waist. "See? Not so bad."

I glared up at him. "Just keep your hands from wandering. Now what do you want to talk about?" His hands snaked lower and I growled. "Keep it up and see where your hands end up next."

Chuckling, he lifted them higher. "I like watching your cheeks blush. It's sexy as hell."

"Will you stop already?" I snapped.

His smile faded, eyes darkening. "Why is it you can

joke around with everyone else, but when I do it you get pissed off?"

"Because they're my friends."

"And I'm not?" he countered, the muscles in his jaw ticking.

Sighing, I tried to pull out of his arms, but he held firm. "You are, but it's not the same." We used to banter quite easily, until the night it all changed between us. I knew what caused the tension, but he'd ignored it and decided it was best to spend his time with other females; at least, up until recently, when I started being around other men. Now he wanted what he couldn't have. Besides all of that, my track record with men wasn't exactly a good one. It was best if I stayed away from falling in love, even if that included my true mate.

"What about my brother? You have no problems joking around with him." For a split second, I could've sworn there was a hint of jealousy in his tone.

My gaze landed on Micah, who paid us no attention, as he was too busy talking to a group of men at the bar. He was Sebastian's doppelganger, but they were nothing alike. For the past couple months, he'd been my sparring partner. The draw to him wasn't there though. "Micah and I train together, Sebastian. That's it."

He nodded toward the door. "That's what I want to talk to you about. Can we go outside?" His gaze bore into mine and I gave in, giving him a nod.

"Fine, let's go."

"You're not going anywhere," a voice teasingly called out. With a wide grin, Colin sauntered up and stood beside Sebastian, who fumed with impatience. I couldn't help but enjoy the tension. I was seeing a side of Sebastian I'd never seen before. "The only place she's going is back on the dance floor with me," Colin said, holding out his hand.

Sebastian glared at him and grabbed my arm. "Maybe another time."

Colin shook his head. "Now will do. You're being summoned," he said, pointing across the room at Bailey and his brother, Micah. "Apparently, they have something important to discuss with you."

Squeezing my hand, Sebastian caught Bailey and Micah's gaze from across the room. He swore under his breath, before he focused on me. "We'll continue this later." Glaring at Colin one more time, he took off across the room.

Colin watched him leave in a huff, then turned to me, smiling devilishly. "Nothing ever changes, does it? For as long as I've known him, he's always been territorial. Now, how about that dance?" He held out his hand and I reluctantly took it.

I could feel the heat of Sebastian's gaze on us as Colin twirled me around the dance floor and pulled me into his arms. He knew what he was doing. "Do you like pissing people off?" I asked.

"Only when they stand in the way of something I want. You don't have feelings for him do you?" I shook my head, hoping like hell he couldn't tell it was a lie. Smiling, he held me closer. "Good. He's a little old for you."

Laughing, I shook my head. "How old do you think I am?"

He studied me, narrowing his gaze in concentration as he looked into my eyes. "Well, I'll be damned. You're just as old as him, aren't you?"

"Maybe not over a hundred, but I'm up there. It's nice being able to look like I'm in my twenties. I'm not going to complain."

His smile grew wider. "What can I say? I love older women."

Sebastian's eyes flashed at hearing this, but I paid him no mind. "What are you doing tomorrow night?" I asked.

"Hopefully, spending time with you," he replied smoothly. "Do you have something in mind?"

I did, but it was going to piss a certain wolf off. Maybe then he'd know what it felt like to be in my position.

TWO

SEBASTIAN

"Why in the fuck of all fucks did you have to call me over now?" I growled.

My brother tried to hide his chuckle, but Bailey slapped him on the arm and addressed me. "I knew what you were going to tell her and I don't think it's the right time. She'll get angry."

I threw my hands in the air. "Why?" Tyla needed to know everything was about to change, whether she liked it or not.

Bailey sighed. "Trust me, I'm a female and I know how Tyla's going to take the news. Just leave her alone for tonight."

All I could see was red as I watched Colin touch her and swing her around the dance floor. She had on a dress that showed off her long legs, and her blonde curls were pulled back away from her face. I'd wanted to wrap my hands in those curls for months. If Colin wasn't Bailey's brother, I'd have ripped off his hands by now.

"So I'm supposed to just let her go off with your brother and do whatever the hell she wants?" I snapped.

Shrugging, she glanced at them quickly and then back to me. "Colin likes her, Sebastian. At least he has enough sense to tell her. You can only blame yourself if she chooses him. Not to mention, she's no young pup. You can't just go in demanding shit and expect her to accept it."

Clenching my teeth, I stood there, blood boiling. Colin was not her mate. "Out of all the females in this pack, why did he have to pick her?"

Micah slapped me on the arm. "Because we always want the ones we can't have, brother. You don't seem to have problems fucking any of the other women you come across."

I hadn't had sex with anyone since I'd come to Wyoming. I couldn't help it everyone assumed I was fucking everyone under the sun. My guess was, Tyla thought the same thing as well. No wonder she didn't want to have anything to do with me. "You all don't know shit," I said, shaking my head.

Tyla and Colin left to go outside and I took a step forward, determined to catch her before she left with him. There was no way in hell I was going to let them be alone.

"Seb, wait!" Micah called. I kept going and didn't stop. What was it about her that drove me absolutely insane? I could feel my control slipping the more she was around. I didn't get to the door in time before a set of arms wrapped around my waist from behind.

"Where you running off to so fast? You seem to have a habit of doing that." Her name was Jana, a gray wolf from the Northwestern pack. She'd been trying to get me into bed with her for months, but I wasn't interested. It's a good thing she was great at playing poker, as it's the only part of her company I enjoyed from time to time.

Grasping her wrists, I tried to pry her away without hurting her, but she latched on tight. "Let me go, Jana. I need to get out of here."

"Why don't I come with you? We could have some fun." She was drunk, alcohol saturating her breath.

Tyla chose then to come marching back into the bar, stopping cold when she saw us, her fiery gaze staring at the woman's arms around my waist. Jaw clenched, she turned and stormed out the door again.

"Goddammit!" I growled, my anger slicing through the room like a knife.

Jana immediately let go and backed away, scared. I could smell her fear. Sighing, I turned around and faced her. Her light brown hair was in one long braid down the side and her eyes tore right through me.

"Shit, I'm sorry, Jana. I don't know what came over me." It was a lie. I knew what my problem was.

She forced a smile and stepped back into Ian, alpha of her pack. Eyes narrowed, he studied me, recognition flashing in his gaze. "You okay, Sebastian?" Ian knew what it felt like to have the darkness inside of him. It was what us unmated males called 'the rage,' an unfortunate side effect of not being mated early on in life.

"I just need some air." By now everyone was watching me. Turning on my heel, I stormed outside and took a deep breath. How long was I going to be able to fight it?

"Looking for me?" Tyla called out, her anger focused

right on me. She crossed her arms and leaned against the side of the building.

"Where's Colin?"

"He left." Luckily, it was without her. "Now what do you want?"

Bailey had warned me not to say anything tonight. As much as I wanted to protest, she was probably right. "I don't think tonight's the right time," I said. "What are you doing tomorrow night?"

A mischievous smile spread across her face. "Colin and I have a date. I'm sure Jana will be more than happy to spend time with you if you're lonely."

I'd thought I had the rage inside of me tamped down, but I was wrong; it came back with a vengeance. "There's nothing going on between me and Jana. Are you pissed because you saw her with me in there?" I nodded toward the bar.

She shrugged flippantly. "That's your own business, Sebastian. I'm not your warden. I don't give a flying fuck who you sleep with."

I stalked toward her and she stood firm. "That's a lie and you know it."

She scoffed. "I swear, you and the other royals think the world revolves around you."

"Is that what you truly think?"

Her gaze focused on something over my shoulder and her expression softened. Sighing, she stepped away from the wall, her steps slowly retreating. "No, not all of you, just certain ones. I've gotta go." She took off down the street and I started to go after her, but a hand to my shoulder stopped me. I knew who it was.

"Leave me be, brother," I warned.

Micah gripped harder. "Let her go, Seb. It's not going to do you any good. Tyla's extremely stubborn. You're only pushing her away."

"Then what the hell am I supposed to do?"

"First," he said, circling around to face me, "how long have you been feeling the rage? It has some of the elders concerned. In fact, you had everyone on edge back there."

I sighed. "I have it under control."

"Didn't look like it a few minutes ago. Besides, that's not what I asked. How long?"

Clenching my teeth, I looked straight into his eyes. "Since I moved here."

"And sleeping with women doesn't help?"

"I haven't slept with anyone since I've been here."

His eyes went wide. "You mean to tell me you haven't fucked a single woman in this city? How the hell is that possible?"

"Simple. I don't put my dick in them."

"That's what you need though. It might not get rid of the rage, but it will help keep it to a simmer. Is it Tyla you want?" He didn't know she was my true mate. No one knew, other than me and Tyla.

Averting my gaze, I focused on the street down which she disappeared. My body fought against me, desperate to track her down. "I can't seem to think of anyone but her. I didn't realize it was going to be like this." Micah tried to hide his smile and failed. "What?" I growled.

"Why don't you come over early in the morning? Tyla will be by to spar with me. If you're up for it, I think I have a plan."

THREE

TYLA

"I want to try something new with you today," Micah hollered from across the yard. "Just give me a sec." He rushed inside, the screen door slamming shut behind him.

I bent down and stretched while I waited on him. Every morning before I went to work, Micah would help me train. I knew how to fight, but he had the skills of a warrior. I'd had the chance to fight alongside him before, and when he offered to help me, I couldn't refuse. At the time, I'd hoped it'd be Sebastian asking me, but it never happened.

I had no clue what the hell his problem was. He only wanted me now because Colin wanted me too. Typical male bullshit.

Micah rushed out of his house and joined me in the pasture. "You ready, T?"

I looked down at his hand, where he held a piece of black cloth. "What's that for?"

Grinning wide, he walked behind me and tied it around

my eyes. I couldn't see a thing. "We're going to spar like this today. One day, you might have to fight using only a few of your senses. I want to see how well you'll do."

"Great," I grumbled. Everything grew quiet, except for the birds chirping and the wind blowing through the trees. I know I looked like an idiot standing there twiddling my thumbs. A minute passed and then another. "When are we going to start?" I asked, lifting my hands in the air. There was no reply.

I was about to rip my blindfold off when my legs were swiped out from underneath me, and I fell hard to the ground, the breath whooshing out of my lungs. I gasped for air and shouted, "You're gonna pay for that, Lyall."

Laughing, Micah tried to take me down again, but I was prepared and jumped out of the way. "Good job. You're learning fast," he praised.

I crouched low and waited for him to strike again. "I knew you'd be impressed. Now give me what you got." He rushed by me and I tried to hit him and missed. Several times he did the same move, but he was too fast for me to catch. *I can do this.* Taking a deep breath, I blocked out every other sound and listened for his steps. The second I heard the whoosh of air, I went on the attack. He tried to grab me, but I side-stepped him and smacked him on the back of the head. I burst out laughing when he growled.

"Didn't expect that, did you?" I teased.

I thought he'd throw back a cutting comment, but there was only the sound of his rapid breathing. Before I could throw another cocky comment his way, he lunged and almost knocked me down to the ground, but I caught myself and got away. His movements were more aggressive and sporadic than usual. What the hell was going on?

My thoughts made me lose focus. Micah clutched me around the waist and we toppled to the ground. I tried to fight him off, but he grabbed my wrists and held them above my head, his legs straddling my waist. I could feel his breath on my face getting hotter as his body moved closer.

"Micah, what are you doing?" He moved down over me until our chests were touching, his breath on my lips. "Stop," I commanded. Only he didn't. As soon as our lips connected, his power blasted into me and I couldn't fight back; my body didn't want to. I knew it was Sebastian. The asshole had no right!

Once he stopped kissing me, the spell broke and I could move away. Growling, I jerked my wrists out of his grasp and pushed him off as hard as I could. He grunted as his body hit the ground.

"What the fuck are you doing?" I shouted, ripping the blindfold off. I jumped to my feet and glared at him. I wanted to hate him, but I couldn't. It was a good thing I was great at acting.

Sebastian brushed the grass off of his pants and T-shirt. At first, he looked exactly like Micah, but it didn't take long for me to realize he was wearing Micah's clothing. Sebastian always wore top notch clothes and stayed perfectly kempt all day. Never was his hair in disarray like it was now. Taking in his appearance, I realized I liked it; I wanted to run my fingers through his messy hair. *What the fuck am I saying?*

He held up his hands. "It was the only way I knew I

could get you alone. Just don't be mad at my brother." Micah was lucky he was nowhere to be seen.

Huffing, I straightened my clothes, patience running thin. "Oh, I'm not worried about him. I'll pay him back tomorrow. You, on the other hand, had no fucking right. Aren't you a little long in the tooth to enjoy playing games?"

Collecting himself, Sebastian stood and blew out a heavy sigh. "I'm not playing games, Tyla. I just needed you to see."

"See what?" I shouted.

He stepped forward. "You're my true mate. I just never acted upon it until now."

I snorted. "You mean you were too busy fucking around with other women to give me the time of day." His eyes flashed but I held up my hand. "I don't want to hear it, Sebastian. I get it, you're a hot commodity, with women falling at your feet every step you take. So excuse me if I don't follow suit. What I'm feeling right now is lust and nothing more. You're not my mate . . . because I don't want you to be."

Eyes burning, I turned around and ran straight to my car. It was all lies, and my bluff was as thin as rice paper. My wolf wanted to be claimed by her mate; I just refused to give in. Knowing what happened to the men I fell in love with, I couldn't go through it again. I'd made a vow and I was determined to keep it.

"What's wrong?" Blake asked, coming up behind me.

Blake Evans was my boss and a friend of the Royal Pack, even though he had no clue we were wolves. He was an undercover cop and I was sure he'd be able to find out what we were if he had any suspicions. That was how good he was at figuring people out. I'd worked for his grandfather when he was alive and now that Blake took over the ranch, I worked for him.

"Earth to Tyla. You goin' to answer me?"

I finished brushing down Blake's horse, Nightshade, and wiped my eyes. My chest ached and I had no clue what I was going to do about it. "I'm fine."

"Does it have to do with Sebastian? I heard it through the grapevine he got mighty pissed when he saw you with someone else."

Gasping, I jerked around. "Who told you that?"

A small smile spread across his face. "I ran into Bailey at

the grocery store this morning. I told her I was sorry I couldn't be at the party last night."

"And she just happened to tell you what was going on?"

He bit his lip. "Colin was with her. Of course, he was more than happy to let it slip."

"Great," I grumbled, turning back to Nightshade. "Can we please not talk about my love life?"

Laughing, he patted Nightshade's backside. "Sure thing. I just wanted to make sure you were all right. I'd hate to have to kick some ass."

"Thanks, boss. You know I can handle it though." He might be exceptionally strong for a human, but he would never be able to handle a wolf.

Once I was done with Nightshade, it was time for me to go. I said my goodbyes and reluctantly headed home. I knew once the sun dipped behind the mountains, Colin would be showing up for our date; a midnight run to the lake. And everything would've been fine for our date if Sebastian hadn't kissed me earlier. It'd changed everything; throwing my need to mate into high gear.

When I got to my house, I could sense Sebastian was near, but ignored it. Maybe if I ignored the signs they'd go away? Yeah, right.

Night came all too quickly, and of course, Colin showed up on time. When I answered the door, he smiled. "You ready?"

A blast of power swept over me; Sebastian was angry. I glanced up at Colin, but he didn't seem to notice, only smiling wider. Okay, so maybe he did know and was eating it up. I was surprised neither of them had pissed on me yet.

"Let's go," I said, shutting the door behind me.

My house was hidden behind a mass of trees, making it easy to shift and run deep into the woods. He followed me around to the back, where we took off our clothes and draped them over the porch banister. Once he shifted into his massive white wolf, he took off into the woods.

I hung back, trying to sense where Sebastian was. He was gone; I couldn't feel him anymore. Colin's howl sounded off in the distance so I quickly shifted and raced after him. It felt good to run free.

We reached the lake and shifted back, the moon glowing across the water. Colin sat down on the ground and patted the space beside him. "Sit down with me."

I sat down and kept my gaze on the lake, waiting for the moment I'd feel Sebastian's power. Colin turned his body toward me. He'd been in the pack for a month but I'd never really spoken to him. "How do you like being in Wyoming?" I asked.

He glanced out at the mountains in the distance and shrugged. "It's different. Don't get me wrong, I love being with my family, but having so many unmated alphas in one pack is an absolute nightmare."

I snorted. "You're telling me."

Smirking, he leaned back on his elbows, stretching out his body. I had to admit, he had a nice one. "So, how come a beautiful woman like you hasn't found a mate yet?"

"I don't know," I laughed. "Why haven't you?"

"Looking in all the wrong places, I guess. That'll change soon."

I didn't want to comment, so I just sat there, smiling uncomfortably. Why had I asked him out? My wolf stirred impatiently inside. She didn't want to be with Colin. Her tastes preferred a different royal.

"I heard you work on a ranch, training horses and such. Do you like it?"

Breathing a sigh of relief, I smiled. Now *that* was a subject I was comfortable with. "Love it. I can't imagine doing anything else. My goal in life was to be a veterinarian, but my family didn't have the money to send me to college. I could probably go now, but I'm more than happy where I'm at."

Colin nodded in understanding. "I didn't go to college either, but Zayne taught me how to design and build houses. We made pretty decent money up in Canada. I'm hoping to start expanding our business down into the states soon."

Zayne was one of Sebastian's brothers, but I'd only met him for a brief moment when he'd arrived in town with Colin and others from what used to be the Royal pack. Zayne was identical to Sebastian and Micah, but he didn't talk nearly as much. I think I'd only heard him say two things since he'd been in the pack.

"Builders are always needed around here," I mentioned.

His lips pulled back into a grin. "I know. I've been hired to work at Three Bar Ranch for maintenance repairs."

Eyes wide, I gaped at him. Surely, he had the name of the ranch wrong. "You know that's where I work, right?"

"Yep. I wasn't going to tell you, but I thought better of it and decided to mention it before I showed up over there tomorrow."

"Thanks for the heads up."

"No problem. Want to go for a swim before we head back?" he asked, smirking mischievously.

Instead of replying, I jumped off the ground and raced toward the water. "First one there wins."

His power flared behind me as he drew near, chuckling the entire time. I was almost to the water's edge when his arms snaked around my waist and pulled me back as we both dove in. His hold loosened and I swam away.

The moment I surfaced, I broke out in laughter. "I won!"

Colin wiped the water out of his eyes. "Don't think so, sweetheart. My arm hit before any other part of your body."

"You're really going to use that bullshit excuse? I can't wait to tell everyone what a sore loser you are."

His eyes flashed and he chuckled. "We'll see about that." He stalked toward me, kicking water in the air as he approached. Squealing, I took off further into the lake, treading as fast as I could. His hand brushed my foot, before he grabbed my ankle, pulling me back toward him. "Who's the faster one now?" he teased, wrapping his arms around my waist.

He was so close, I felt his breath on my face. Even if he kissed me, I knew it wouldn't feel anything like Sebastian's kiss from earlier. "Colin," I whispered regretfully.

"You don't have to say it, Tyla. I know I'm not the one you want. Although, I have to say, it kills me not to kiss you right now."

Sighing, I hung my head. "I didn't want to lead you on, but I was hoping my feelings would change. They haven't, and I'm sorry. The last thing you need is to get on Sebastian's bad side."

He chuckled. "I think I already am. I'm not worried about it."

He should be though.

FOUR

SEBASTIAN

Who the fuck does he think he is? I didn't want Tyla to know I was watching, but dammit to hell, it was getting hard to control myself. I wanted to rip Colin's throat out every time he touched her. Now they were in the lake and way too fucking close. *That's it.* I started toward them, my resolve on the edge of breaking.

"Don't even think about it, Sebastian."

I stopped and turned around to find Bailey glaring at me, her heart racing from the run. It was easier to control our emotions in human form; hence, the reason I refrained from shifting. "What the hell are you doing here?" She'd shielded herself so I wouldn't hear or feel her approach.

Arms crossed, she stood there, pursing her lips. "Micah sent me to get you. He thought you'd rip his head off if he came, and we both know you won't hurt me. Judging by what's going on, you better not hurt Colin either."

My eyes flashed. "She doesn't belong to him. He needs to stop touching her."

Sighing, she approached cautiously. "He knows that. Colin isn't going to make a move on Tyla, I promise."

"Have you *seen* them out there?" I growled, thrusting my finger in their direction.

"You have nothing to worry about. My plan worked. However, I'm starting to think it was a mistake."

"Plan? What the fuck are you going on about?"

Her gaze landed on Tyla and Colin, who were finally emerging from the lake. "Colin is only pursuing Tyla because I asked him to. He's not actually trying to steal her away; he's just making it *appear* as if he's doing so. I knew you needed a push and he's the only one crazy enough to take you on."

"You have got to be kidding me. Why would you do that? I could've ripped him apart," I snapped.

She stepped forward. "That's why I'm intervening now. I didn't realize you were having such a hard time controlling yourself."

"Is Tyla in on this?"

"No," she said with a shake of her head. "It won't matter anyway. We both know she's not interested in Colin. You're her mate and she knows that, even as pig-headed as she is being."

I huffed. "And that's what drives me so crazy. She fights me every second she gets."

"You deserve it. I can't help it you're an idiot. Now's the time to make it up to her."

I could hear Tyla's laugh from where I stood. She used to be carefree like that around me, until I'd started flaunting other women around her, hoping the feelings would stop. In the end, they only grew worse. I focused on her, the way she smiled so animatedly at Colin. Would she ever smile like that at me again?

"She hates me." I sighed and looked at the ground. "I tricked her today and made her kiss me. You know as well as I that she's not the forgiving type. The longer she fights me, the worse I'll get."

She placed her hand on my shoulder. "That's why you need to be honest with her. It's either that, or find someone else to control your urges with for the time being. But that option will only piss her off more, so . . ."

I groaned, angrily running a hand through my hair. "I always knew a woman would be the death of me."

"And a hell of a one at that." Bailey laughed. "Now, come on back to my house. Ryker and I need your help." She squeezed my shoulder.

"Fine, but if I find out your brother makes a move on her, I'll rip his balls off. Got it?"

She snickered. "Colin may like to fuck with you, but he knows his limits, and so does Tyla. She doesn't want him."

"She may not want him, but it doesn't mean she won't use him to get back at me. I fucked up, and deserve whatever she decides to throw my way."

Bailey didn't say a word, which meant I was absolutely right. Out of the hundred years I'd lived in this godforsaken world, you'd think I'd have learned by now. *Obviously not.*

By the time we got back to her house, I could hear Ryker cursing up a storm inside. "What the hell is he doing?" I asked, holding back a chuckle.

Bailey cleared her throat. "When Micah came over to talk to me, he told me you helped my parents put my crib together. I thought maybe you could help put my little one's together as well. Ryker seems to need some help."

More cursing ensued and I chuckled. I'd do anything to get my mind off of Tyla. "I'd be happy to. When your mother was pregnant with you, I knew you were going to be a handful, always moving around like a beast."

She stopped at the door. "Do you regret choosing to be a protector?"

"No. It's what my father did, and his before that for several generations. The legacy needs to live on. So far, we haven't failed in our tasks." Then I thought about Tyla. "At least, until I picked the most stubborn female on this planet to protect."

She giggled. "Whether Tyla realizes it or not, you're her mate, a man who has sworn to protect her. Any female in our pack would kill to have you as their protector."

"All except her," I scoffed.

Ryker ripped open the front door and huffed, his eyes flashing. "Somebody better help me soon, before I toss this crib onto the lawn. The instructions are pure garbage."

Bailey nudged me with her elbow and I cleared my throat to keep from laughing. "Step aside, Whitemore. I've got this." I walked in and shook my head at the mess on the floor. There were pieces of the crib strewn everywhere. Ryker picked up the instructions and handed them to me, but I waved him off. "Don't need them."

Minutes later, I had the crib put together, grinning triumphantly.

"Hats off to you, Lyall," Ryker said, leaning against the couch. "I think this calls for a beer."

Bailey rolled her eyes and sat down on the couch while

I followed Ryker into the kitchen. As soon as he passed me a beer, a knock sounded on the door.

"I'll get it," Bailey called.

Colin's voice filtered into the house and my back stiffened. Biting my tongue, I tried my best to control my temper.

"What's up?" he asked, strutting into the kitchen. He didn't look surprised to see me in the least.

Ryker passed him a beer and slapped his shoulder. "Just talking to Lyall here." Clearing his throat, he turned to me, amused at the tension. "I'll be in the living room if you need me."

Colin gulped his beer and leaned over on the counter, his gaze fixed on mine. "I know you were there tonight," he stated matter-of-factly.

I slammed my bottle on the counter. "*And?*"

He huffed. "I'm sure Bailey told you already. It was all an act. I wasn't going to make Tyla do anything she didn't want to do. Lucky for you, she's not into me."

My wolf stirred impatiently. All he wanted was to punish the guy for touching his mate. What the hell was I saying? She wasn't even my fucking mate yet. I drank the rest of my beer and tossed my bottle in the trash.

"For future reference, keep your hands to yourself. I can't promise you'll have them if you touch her again." I walked out of the room and heard his chuckle behind me. But I wasn't kidding.

It was early the next day, and I wanted to catch Tyla before she left for the ranch. When I arrived, she was already pulling out of her driveway for the day, but headed the opposite way from the ranch. Where was she going?

She drove south, about forty-five minutes away from Jackson Hole, until she stopped at the entrance to Pineview Cemetery. Following her in, I parked down the street and watched as she got out of her car. Weaving her way through the graves, she stopped at one and sat down. I didn't dare follow her any closer, but I watched her from a distance, listening.

"Happy Birthday, Cliff," she said in a shaky voice. "You would've been forty-eight years old today." She rubbed her hand over the gravestone. "I miss you so much. Everything was less complicated when you were around. Don't get me wrong, I'm happy. I just . . ." She paused and blew out a sigh. "I'm afraid. And I don't know what to do."

Leaning over the gravestone, her shoulders shook as she cried. I wanted to go to her, to put my arm around her and tell her everything would be okay, but I couldn't let her know I was there.

For the next ten minutes, she sat there, her cries being all I could hear. Then her phone rang and she gasped, wiping her eyes quickly before answering. "Amelie, what's up?" I could hear the rapid breath of the female on the other end.

"*Tyla, help!*" Amelie shouted. "*I don't know how long I can last.*" She screamed and the sound of growling wolves echoed in the phone before everything went dead.

"Amelie? What's going on? Amelie!" Tyla screamed. She hung up and shot to her feet.

She kissed the gravestone and placed her hand on top. "I'll come back soon, Cliff."

Whoever this guy was, he had meant something to her. But that was a question for later. Right now, there were bigger problems.

FIVE

I'd called my mother and she'd notified the pack. By the time I got to my parents' house, Bailey and Ryker were already there, along with Colin, Micah, and Cedric, Ryker's second-in-command. The only person missing was Sebastian. I was shocked he wasn't already there. When my mother watched me slam through the door, the look on her face terrified me. She was scared.

"Anything new?" I asked, rushing toward her.

She shook her head. "Nothing good. I've tried calling Sara and Benjamin but they're not picking up." My aunt and uncle always picked up the phone. Bile rose in the back of my throat. What if we didn't get to them in time?

"What are we going to do?" I asked, glancing around the room. Their grim expressions did little to help ease the situation.

Sebastian came storming through the door, his heated gaze fixed on mine. "I can have a couple of my men leave tonight to investigate," he offered.

My parents glanced at each other and my father nodded. "I'll go with them."

"No," I shrieked. Everyone jerked their attention to me and the room fell silent. Sighing, I placed a hand on my dad's shoulder. He was still a strong wolf, but he wasn't the same warrior he used to be; while I had fought battles for years, and had nothing to lose. I was ready.

With my head held high, I turned my attention to Ryker. "I'll go. It's my responsibility."

"Absolutely not," my mother growled. She tried to step in front of me, but I blocked her path.

"Ryker, you know I can do this. You can't send my father out there. I'm stronger and faster than he is."

Before my parents could argue, Sebastian stepped forward. "I'll go with her. I can use my magic to shield us. No one will know we're there. If you send a bunch of wolves, it'll only draw unwanted attention."

Heart racing, I sucked in a breath. Being alone with Sebastian and traveling across the United States would be a disaster. We'd spend the entire time fighting each other. I'd end up killing him. How in the hell was that going to help my family?

He kept his eyes on mine as we waited for the final verdict. Not that Ryker could control what Sebastian did, but it was more of a show of respect for Bailey.

Time seemed to stand still as Ryker glanced around the room and then bowed his head in a final nod. "It's done," he said. Sebastian stepped up to him and they shook hands. "I have no doubt you'll know what to do. Keep her safe."

Sebastian glanced over at me. "With my life."

Just hearing the words made me shiver. Tearing my gaze

away, I faced my parents. My father beamed with pride, but my mother was terrified.

"Why are you doing this?" she asked.

"Why wouldn't I? When my family is attacked, it's my job to help them. You know I can do this. I'm a stronger fighter than most of the men in our pack." Cedric snorted from across the room and I flipped him off. The others laughed, as Ryker shooed them from the house, except for Bailey and Sebastian.

"I know you're a good fighter, sweetheart," my mother said, "but you're putting yourself in danger. You don't know what you'll be up against."

I ruffled her curls and smiled. "The only thing you have to worry about is me killing Sebastian. Other than that, I'll be fine."

A sad smile spread across her lips. "We both know that's not going to happen," she whispered softly, placing a gentle kiss on my cheek. I stiffened and could feel his penetrating gaze on my back. "Now, behave. He needs you more than you know." She'd said it like there was something I didn't know. What was she keeping from me?

She pulled away and my father wrapped his arms around me while my mother disappeared into the kitchen. "Be careful, Tyla." He kissed the top of my head and let go.

My mother came back and handed me a piece of paper. "I don't know if Amelie told you where they lived, but here are the addresses to her place and her parents'."

I nodded and hugged her tight. "I'll find them."

She sniffled and squeezed. "I know you will."

"Tyla, we should probably go," Sebastian suggested, his voice achingly close.

Nodding, I took a deep breath and followed him outside. Ryker and the others were there, waiting on us.

"Seb," Micah shouted, waving Sebastian over to where he was standing with Ryker.

"I'll only be a minute," he murmured. As soon as he walked off, Bailey joined me.

We watched on as Sebastian walked over to Micah and Ryker, their voices so low I couldn't hear them. I leaned over toward Bailey. "What do you think they're saying?"

She put her arm around me and walked me to my car. "Ryker's telling him he needs to calm down. He's too volatile."

"I can tell. Why is he like that? It's not normal for Sebastian."

She lowered her gaze and sighed. "You know what happens when a male goes too long without his mate, right?"

Mouth gaping, I felt like I'd been sucker punched in the gut. "You're serious? How long has he been fighting it?" I knew what men did to curve the cravings for their mate. There was no telling how many women he'd slept with to ease his rage. That was probably why I had no clue he was struggling.

"A few months now. It gets worse when he sees you with another male." My gaze drifted back to Sebastian and I could see it in his stance; he was tense. Bailey snapped her fingers in front of my face. "This is serious, Tyla. He could snap and go completely off the deep end. You can't keep provoking him. *You* are his mate. Whatever issues you have between the two of you, you need to work them out, and soon."

Sebastian shook Ryker's hand and started toward me. "I wish I could," I murmured, swallowing down the regret. "But there's nothing I can do. I'm cursed."

She started to speak, but Sebastian jumped in. "How long will it take you to pack?" he asked.

I shrugged. "Fifteen minutes."

He nodded. "All right. I'll reserve our plane tickets and meet you at your house."

Bailey hugged him and gave him a look I couldn't decipher, before he turned around and got in his car. Why did it feel like everyone was keeping secrets from me?

I knew he was close by the thrumming in my veins. It was one of the first mating signs I'd experienced. Since my parents were true mates, I knew what to expect. For the longest time, I had tried to convince myself I'd felt them when I was with Finn, but it had just been wishful thinking.

Now, I know why I never felt them. My wolf had been waiting for Sebastian.

He knocked on the door and I wanted to kick myself in the ass for being filled with excitement. He'd be able to hear my heart pounding through the door. When I opened it, he stepped inside. "You ready? Our flight to Nashville leaves in an hour."

"Nashville? Why are we going there?"

"It was either that, or stop in Denver for a five hour layover. Nashville made more sense. From there we can drive to Cherokee, North Carolina. I knew you'd want to get there as fast as we could." For once, he wasn't being a smart ass, but genuine.

"Thanks," I replied.

My bags were on the floor and I was about to pick them up when he grabbed my wrist. "I got them." He let me go and picked up my bags.

I loved the way his muscles flexed and tightened when he threw them over his shoulder. Blowing out a sigh, I reluctantly averted my gaze. I seriously needed to get a better handle on the situation. "Let me grab my keys and I'll be ready," I called out to him.

As he was putting the bags in the car, I stayed inside to catch my breath. Being around him was going to be a lot harder than I thought.

SIX

"W ant to go for a run?" Bailey asks as I open the door. I glance behind her at the rest of the females from our pack, undressing on my lawn.

"What's going on? I thought you'd be with Ryker."

A wide grin spreads across her face. "And I will be, if he manages to catch me. We're doing something new tonight. I thought it'd be fun. Now come on!" She grabs my hand and pulls me outside. The others have already shifted and their excitement is palpable.

I take off my shirt and toss it on the ground. "Are we playing hide and seek or something?" I joke.

Bailey smirks. "Something like that. Since our magic is running high with the full moon, I thought a game would be fun. The guys are all at my house getting ready. When Ryker howls, it will start. They'll be coming after us."

I scoff. "So we're just supposed to let them chase us? Where's the fun in that?" I've never been the type of girl to run away. I like to fight.

She leans closer, whispering in my ear. "We're alpha females, Tyla. The other girls love the chase too, but I'm going to make Ryker work for it."

"Then I pity who comes after me. I'm not going to make it easy on them."

"That's the spirit." She laughs. "Maybe Sebastian will chase after you. You two seem to be finding your way to each other a lot. Every time I turn around, there you are. What's up with that?"

"He's fun to talk to." I shrug. "I can't help it we run into each other all the time."

She shakes her head, clearly not believing me at all. There's no denying I'm attracted to Sebastian, but he's a player. Women constantly follow him around. His brother, Micah, would be more my style. He's down to earth and easy-going, something Sebastian isn't.

Ryker's howl echoes in the air, followed by the other males. Bailey beams and turns to the girls. "It's time. Let's have some fun." The others take off into the woods as Bailey and I finish undressing. "Good luck, Tyla."

"Same to you."

We shift and sprint in opposite directions. The energy is high all around us and it's euphoric. The idea of a chase is brilliant. Most of the guys in my pack won't pick me to chase though. They know they'll lose. If all else fails, I'm prepared to enjoy the full moon on my own. Slowing my pace, I stop by the lake and dip a paw into the water. In another month or so it'll be frozen over.

There isn't a wolf around for miles, proving my point— no one is going to come after me. Shifting back into my human form, I walk the rest of the way into the water and swim out toward the middle. There are many times I'll sneak away in the dead of night to take a swim. It's the only time I can find peace. Floating on my back, I peer up at the glowing moon; it's enchantingly beautiful. At least, until a set of arms come up from the water and I scream. My screams are cut off as I'm pulled down into the dark depths, sucking in a mouthful of water.

I can hear a muffled laugh, and I know exactly who it is. As soon as he lets me go, I shoot up out of the water and growl. "I am so going to kill you. You scared the shit out of me." I splash him in the face and he laughs even harder.

"That was priceless. I thought for sure you heard me jump in the water." Sebastian circles around me.

"Clearly, I didn't. Just know that payback's a bitch."

He splashes water at me this time. "You should've been paying attention. What if it wasn't me coming after you?"

I roll my eyes and splash him again. "Most do not have the ability to shield their presence. Why did you hide anyway? Scared I might attack?"

His blue eyes flash and it makes me shiver. "I just wanted to watch you. You're different when you're by yourself."

"How so?"

He shrugs. "Not sure yet, but it's kind of like you're a million miles away."

He's absolutely right. "Sometimes I am. When I'm alone, I can't help but think about the past."

"Want to talk about it? We can go downtown and grab a couple of drinks. It'll be my repentance for scaring you."

"Sounds like a great idea. Let's go." I've refrained from talking about my past, but maybe it's time to let it out. He *grabs my hand to lead me out and at that point, everything changes.*

His eyes glow and I pull away from his touch. I look up at the moon and want to curse it. "This can't be happening," I murmur. Sebastian tries to reach for me again but I throw up my hand. "Don't."

"But you felt it . . ."

I shake my head quickly. "It doesn't mean anything. Every time I . . ." I start to tell him my fears and then stop. "I'm sorry . . . this isn't going to work." Without another word, I shift and race off into the woods, ignoring his call for me to wait.

The next day, I try to approach him, but he's too busy with two human females at the bar to notice me. It's like I don't even exist. I deserve it after leaving him at the lake, but it still doesn't change anything.

"Tyla, wake up," Sebastian murmured in my ear. I jerked awake and sat up. His arm was around me, but he moved it quickly. "Bad dream?"

I looked out the airplane window and could see the lights on the runway. We'd landed already. Thank God we were almost off the plane. He was too close. "You have no idea," I said.

SEVEN

SEBASTIAN

Tyla didn't have to tell me what she'd dreamed about, because she talked in her sleep and had said the exact thing she'd said to me that night at the lake, "I'm sorry . . . this isn't going to work." Those words had plagued my mind ever since they slipped from her lips. Watching her walk away from me that night was the most infuriating thing, and I did what was necessary to ease that tension. I drank. It was the only thing that dulled the nagging ache of rejection.

I was her mate. Why was she fighting it?

Once we got off the plane, I rented a black SUV, then we were on our way to the mountains of North Carolina. Tyla was right beside me, but she might as well have been a thousand miles away. Why did she have to be so goddamned stubborn?

"Why don't you tell me about Amelie? What is your family doing all the way out here and not in Wyoming with you and your parents?" I asked, hoping to strike up some conversation.

Sighing, she leaned her head against the seat, refusing to look at me. I'd give anything to look into those gray eyes of hers. "Amelie's my cousin. We're the same age. When our pack was attacked many years ago, we all went our separate ways. Instead of coming with us, my aunt and uncle felt safer going rogue. That way, they could travel wherever they wanted and stay hidden. Amelie went with them and I haven't seen her since."

"Who attacked your pack?" I asked.

She shrugged. "A psychotic wolf in search of a mate."

"What happened to everyone else in your pack? Where are they now?"

Her face fell. "I don't know. I'm assuming they're dead." I could feel her pain like a knife to the gut.

"Do your parents not know where they are?"

Closing her eyes, she shook her head. "Can we please stop talking about this? I spent years grieving the loss of my pack. I don't want to think about it anymore. Why don't we talk about something else?"

"I would, if I knew it wouldn't piss you off. It seems everything I do these days makes you angry."

"I guess that's the problem of being you," she grumbled.

I swerved the car off the road and slammed it into park. Grabbing her chin, I turned her toward me. I wanted her to look at me for a change. Eyes wide, she froze in my grasp, before anger took over. "Why are you doing this?" I growled.

Her chest rose up and down with her rapid breaths. "I'm upset. I have a bad habit of saying things and thinking later."

"That's for damn sure." I let her chin go and she sighed.

"It's true, isn't it? How did I not realize it was this bad?"

I could see it in her eyes, she knew. "Are you scared of me?"

She shook her head. "I know you won't hurt me. And if you tried, I'd kick your ass. I just wonder how many women you've slept with to keep you from going insane."

Now it all made sense. She thought I'd been fucking around. I threw my hands in the air. "So *that's* why you're pissed? Why didn't you just ask and save us both the trouble?"

Her jaw tensed. "Don't know, don't care."

"You may not care, but if it helps, I'll happily let you know I haven't slept with anyone since I've been here."

She scoffed. "Who's the liar now? I've seen you with other women."

"Seen, yes. But did I fuck them? No." I stared her down, waiting for her to challenge me. "Besides, you're the one who pushed me away first. I know you're scared of something, and I want to know what it is."

She swallowed hard and blew out a shaky breath. "You wouldn't understand."

The whole back and forth thing was infuriating. Putting the car in gear, I sped back onto the road, my knuckles turning white from gripping the steering wheel. "It's a good thing we have time then. I'm not going anywhere, Tyla. No matter how much you push me away, I'm always going to be there."

She waved me off. "Don't you need to concentrate on keeping Bailey safe?"

"I don't watch after her anymore. I've chosen someone

else to protect." Her head jerked my way and I smiled in answer.

"No," she moaned.

"That's right, love. You're stuck with me for the rest of your life, mated or not."

It wasn't exactly the way I'd wanted to tell her, but she needed to hear it. One way or another, I was going to make her submit. She couldn't fight me for the rest of our lives. Or at least, I hoped to hell she couldn't.

EIGHT

F or once in my life I was stunned into silence. I knew he was telling the truth; I could see it in his eyes. As soon as he stopped at a gas station, I jumped out of the car and rushed inside to the bathroom. I didn't care what time it was, Bailey was going to talk to me.

She answered on the second ring, her voice groggy from sleep. "Tyla?"

"Why didn't you tell me about Sebastian? I can't have him as my protector. He'll drive me insane!"

"That's what mates *do*. Stop fighting it and give in. You'll be much happier. Besides, he could've easily picked another wolf to protect. How would you have felt then?" *Angry. Pissed. Infuriated.* "That's what I thought," she said at my silence. "Not to mention, he went to your parents and asked permission." She snorted. "He's so old-fashioned."

"Oh my God," I groaned. Even my parents knew? It felt like the whole universe was against me. I leaned against the bathroom door and bowed my head. "Have you ever been in love before, Bailey? With someone other than Ryker, I mean."

"No, why?"

"That's what I thought. Well, I have. Twice. And both of them were taken from me. I just can't do it again."

"I'm so sorry, Tyla. I know you don't want to lose another love, but Sebastian is your true mate. You're not going to lose him."

No one could say that for sure. "You don't know that. I'd rather not get attached."

She huffed and I could tell she was getting angry with me. "Suit yourself, but one of these days he's going to lose his mind to the rage. I care about him, Tyla. If you don't want him going off the deep end and possibly being killed by another pack, you're going to have to help him."

"He says he hasn't been with anyone since he's been in Wyoming. What if he's lying to me?"

"What if he's not? You should be able to recognize the truth."

He was telling the truth, but it was so hard to believe. This was Sebastian we were talking about, one of the most highly sought after wolves in our pack. Everyone wanted him. "It's much easier to think of him as a dog," I replied.

"Well, he's not. Wait, scratch that, we all kind of are, just a different breed. He's a good guy though, and very strong. The perfect mate, actually."

"Better not let Ryker hear you say that," I said. Sebastian *would* be the perfect mate. That was what made everything so difficult.

Someone knocked on the door, so I flushed the toilet and turned on the water. "Almost done," I called. "Bailey, I have to go. I'll call you as soon as I figure out what's going on."

"We'll be here."

Hanging up, I hurried outside to where Sebastian stood, waiting by the car. He opened the door for me and stepped out of the way. No matter what, he was always a gentleman.

"How long until we get there?" I asked.

"About an hour, depending on traffic."

Nodding, I got into the car. Before he could shut the door, I stopped it with my hand. "I'm sorry," I blurted out, meeting his gaze.

"For what?"

"For being such a bitch. I know my attitude doesn't help our situation and it definitely won't help us find my family."

His brows furrowed. "What are you saying?"

I shrugged. "I'm saying that from now on I'll stop with the snide comments, unless you deserve them. We need to get along if we're to help my family."

"That's it?" he asked, temper flaring. "You have nothing else to say now that you know the truth?" The last thing I wanted was to infuriate him more, but I couldn't offer what he wanted.

"I don't want to argue, Sebastian. Thank you for clearing up the air, but it still doesn't change anything. I'm not ready to be your mate."

Huffing, he averted his gaze, gripping the edge of the car door. "Something tells me you won't ever be ready."

The tension in the car was so thick it could be cut with a knife. His wolf wanted to claim me and mine wanted to be claimed. My fingers ached to touch him and my body yearned to be beneath his, but I knew if I gave in, I wouldn't be able to stop.

We were almost to my aunt and uncle's house, cruising down their mile long gravel driveway. When their cabin came into view, we saw two cars parked out front. Judging by the car tracks, neither one of them had been moved recently.

I typed Amelie's address into my GPS and waited for it to load. "It says we're two miles from Amelie's."

Sebastian nodded and parked the car. All I wanted was for him to talk to me; he hadn't since we'd left the gas station. He got out of the car and I followed suit. "If they're not here, I say we go through the woods. Their cars haven't been moved in days."

"I noticed that when we pulled in," I said.

Dread settled into the pit of my gut. My aunt and uncle were always traveling, going from place to place. There was no way they'd stay put for a long period of time without driving somewhere. We got closer to the cabin and I picked up both my aunt and uncle's scent, along with a trace of Amelie.

"I don't smell any wolves, other than my family," I pointed out.

Sebastian nodded, then looked toward the door. "Want to go inside?"

There was nothing out of place on the front porch, no smashed windows or signs of forced entry. "Yeah, let's take a look."

He turned the knob and the door opened right up. Sarah and Benjamin's scents were in there, but not strong. My eyes burned when I walked into their living room. Nothing was out of place. Their whole house was filled with nothing but Benjamin's handcrafted furniture, and Sarah's paintings hanging on the wall. I missed them so much.

Sebastian came up behind me. "They don't have any enemies do they?"

On the coffee table sat a wooden wolf figurine. Picking it up, I inspected it and shook my head. "Not that I know of. They're the kindest-hearted wolves I know. They'd do anything to avoid a fight." Benjamin loved his artwork more than fighting and Sarah was the same with her paintings. They were the perfect match.

"Unfortunately, there are a lot of wolves who prey on people like them," Sebastian murmured. He headed toward the back door and took a deep breath when he opened it. "Their trails are stronger out here."

He took off out the door and I rushed after him. He was right. Their scents were stronger, especially in the direction toward Amelie's house. Sebastian stopped at the edge of the woods and waited for me.

"You ready?" he asked, rolling his sleeves up.

I nodded. "Let's go." We took off into the woods, and he stayed by my side as we ran. The closer we got to Amelie's house, the sicker I became. The scent of blood permeated the air and was almost overwhelming as the house came into view.

Sebastian stopped and held out his arm. "Wait. I don't like this."

Neither did I, but I had to get to my family. "They're hurt," I cried, dread settling in the pit of my stomach. "I don't sense any other wolves around."

Taking a deep breath, his eyes flashed as he scanned the area. "I don't either. Stay close."

We approached the cabin, and unlike my aunt and uncle's place, there were definitely signs of forced entry. We walked inside and the place was ransacked, blood every-where. And not just Amelie's. But I couldn't smell the other scents.

"She didn't make it easy on them, whoever they are," he mentioned.

The splatters of blood trailed out the back door, which was wide open. "Should we shift?" I asked.

He peered into the woods and shook his head. A look crossed his face but I couldn't decipher it. "Not yet."

"You know something, don't you? What are you not telling me?"

Sighing, he looked down at my hand and grabbed it. "Are you sure you want to go out there?"

By the look in his eyes, I knew what he was thinking. "You're wrong," I growled in denial. They were still alive; they had to be. I squeezed his hand and he squeezed back, his gaze sad. "Either way, I have to see for myself."

He nodded once and guided me down the patio stairs. I didn't even bother letting go of his hand. I needed his touch, especially now. The smell of blood grew thicker the farther into the woods we traveled. We were close.

"Why would anyone want to hurt them?"

Sebastian shrugged. "I'm guessing they were after Amelie. Maybe a wolf wanted her as a mate and she refused?"

Memories of the battle against Vincent's wolves flashed through my mind. I'd barely gotten out alive. "I know all too well about that," I whispered softly. Brows furrowed, he glanced down at me and started to speak, but then stopped, quickly turning his attention to something in the distance. "What is it?"

His royal abilities far outstretched mine. Everything I could do, he could do three times better. "Death," he said. "Why don't you stay here while I take a look?"

I shook my head, eyes burning. "They're my family, Sebastian."

Still holding my hand, he pulled me the rest of the way. I could hear the bugs flying and the vultures ripping away at flesh. If there was ever a time I didn't want wolf hearing, it was then. Swallowing hard, I averted my gaze, knowing their bodies were right under my nose.

Sebastian blew out an angry breath and bowed his head. "I'm so sorry, Tyla."

The vultures scattered and I gagged. My eyes were blurry, but I could see the carnage as if I was looking through a microscope. Slapping a hand over my mouth, my body shook and I fell to my knees. So many emotions whirled through me, I didn't know which one to hold on to. "Oh my God."

There were four wolves, all dead; pieces of their bodies strewn about. Whoever had killed my family had enjoyed it, and made sure to make them suffer. I prayed Karma would be a bitch.

My aunt and uncle were on the ground. Still in wolf form, they were barely intact and gutted, their insides stretched across the dirt and leaves. The only relief to be found, was that my cousin was not there. It looked like after my family ripped the others apart, there were more that came in and devoured them. I could see their tracks, but couldn't smell them.

"Why can't I smell the other tracks? Is it just me?" I asked.

Sebastian let go of my hand and kneeled, touching the tracks. "No, it's not just you. But there's a reason why."

I turned to him. "Why?"

He huffed, jaw tense. "Magic. Whoever did this doesn't want to be found."

"Magic? Are you talking Maret kind of magic?" Maret was a powerful witch I'd helped kill just a few months back. It had happened during a rescue mission for Bailey. I could still taste the foulness of her blood in my mouth. When Sebastian nodded, I groaned. "I didn't think there were any other witches out there like her."

"There must be."

"Why are they trying to hide?" It made no sense. Wolves were all about territory and making themselves known.

"Don't know, but I sure as hell don't like it," he growled.

"What about Amelie? If she's not here, they had to have taken her. How are we going to find her?"

Amelie wasn't a fighter. When we were younger, she'd been the soft-spoken one who chose to pick flowers and search for beautiful rocks instead of climbing trees and playing in the mud. We were the perfect balance together, and the best of friends. The thought of what was being done to her made me sick. It felt like a rock was being wedged in my throat. I couldn't breathe.

Sebastian clutched my cheeks in his hands, turning my face to his. "Calm down, Tyla. We'll find her, I promise. We just need to track her scent."

I tried to turn to the carnage, but he held me firm. "What about my aunt and uncle? We can't just leave them here."

"We won't. But every second matters. We need to see if we can pick up Amelie's scent and find out where she was taken. We'll have to come back and bury your family later." It was a long shot, considering we couldn't even track the other wolves' scents. But we had to try.

I didn't want to leave my family rotting on the ground, but what choice did I have? Nodding, I placed my hands over his. "Okay, let's go."

NINE

W e'd picked up Amelie's scent pretty easily and followed it away from the carnage. It made no sense why they would leave her scent while masking their own.

"Are you thinking what I'm thinking?" I asked, glancing at Sebastian. "Either they want someone to follow her scent, or they figured she wasn't part of a pack, and therefore, no one would try to find her."

I could tell the wheels in his mind were turning. He was older than me and definitely wiser when it came to tracking. "But why would they mask their own scent then? There's something more going on, and I can't figure it out. It makes no sense," he said.

"What do you suggest we do?"

He pointed in the direction Amelie's scent guided us to. "We keep following."

Ten minutes later, we spotted a backcountry road off into the distance. The footprints and spots of blood stopped at the side of the road, where a set of car tires were ingrained in the dried mud.

"They had this planned," I said, glaring at the tire tracks on the road. "Can you tell what kind of car they were in?"

He shook his head. "Only that it's probably a large SUV or van. There are lots of vehicles with that size of tires."

There were no houses within miles. The chances of someone seeing anything were slim. All I could do was stare at the road, hating myself for not knowing what to do. "What the hell are we going to do now?"

Sebastian came up behind me and put a hand on the back of my neck. His touch made me feel things I didn't want to feel. Biting my lip, I slipped out from underneath his hand, hating the disappointment on his face.

He stepped away, the muscles in his jaw tense. "Our best bet is to go back to Amelie's and search around her house. Maybe there's something we missed, a clue as to who would be after her. You haven't seen her in years, so you have no idea who she was involved with."

I threw up my hands. "And the only people who would be able to help are dead," I said angrily. "What's worse is that I still have to tell my parents. My mother's going to be heartbroken."

Out of the corner of my eye, I watched him reach for me again, before stopping short and clenching his hand into a tight fist. How was I going to handle disappointing him every single second of every day? It hurt to know what I was doing to him.

"Let's bury your aunt and uncle before we call them," he said. "That way, they'll know they're resting in peace."

We were standing in front of Amelie's house, staring at the front door. The burial was complete, and now we had to uncover the whereabouts of my cousin.

"Do you want to take a break, or continue our search and go through Amelie's house?" Sebastian asked, concern etched in his voice.

We didn't have time for breaks. The longer Amelie was gone, the smaller her chance of survival became, especially with the full moon coming up in a week's time. I didn't want to imagine what would happen to her if we didn't find her before then.

"Let's start searching," I replied.

Amelie's room was upstairs and that was the first place I went. Everything was still in perfect order, all bright and airy in light blue and white. It was only the downstairs that was in shambles. I sat down on her bed and pulled a pillow into my lap.

Sebastian came into the doorway and stopped, staring at me.

Taking a deep breath, I gazed around her room and found a picture of us from years ago. We had our arms around each other, smiling from ear to ear in our graduation cap and gowns. Sebastian must've followed my gaze because he walked into the room and picked up the picture.

"You're so beautiful," he murmured, before passing it to me.

I smiled. "Thanks. Amelie is as well." I glanced down at the picture. "All the guys followed her around. She loved breaking hearts."

"What about you?" he asked.

My smile faded when I looked up at him. "My life was a little more complicated than hers. I had more responsibilities." From a young age I'd been slated to be our alpha's mate. Everyone knew I was off limits.

Sebastian's gaze narrowed. "What's that supposed to mean?"

I waved him off. "It's not important." I slid off the bed and put the picture back on her desk. She'd always had little trinkets and colorful stones she'd managed to collect over the years. Her desk was decorated with all sorts of gems.

"What's that?" Sebastian announced from behind. I turned to see what he was referring to. And there, on the corner of the desk, sat a brown leather journal with a smooth blue stone sitting on top. Sebastian stared at it like it had three heads.

"It's just Amelie's journal. Maybe she wrote something that'll help us."

I reached for it and Sebastian shouted, only it was too

late; my hand had already closed over the blue stone. A jolt of electricity surged through my veins and it was as if I was taken away from my body. Sebastian yelled my name, but I couldn't get back to him. I was stuck in a world only I could see.

Memories flashed through my mind, but they weren't my own. They were Amelie's. I could see my aunt and uncle smiling, then it changed to blood. I saw their deaths, heard their screams as the other wolves ripped them apart. I wanted to close my eyes and shut it out, but I couldn't. I was trapped. The voices of the wolves were all jumbled in my mind, but their faces started to come to me. Ever so slowly, they became clearer.

"Tyla!"

Gasping, I was thrust back into my own mind, the blue stone skidding across the floor as Sebastian knocked it out of my hands. He lifted me to my feet, cupping his hands against my cheeks. "What the fuck? Are you okay?" His eyes were wild, flashing back and forth between human and wolf.

I nodded quickly. "I'm fine. I don't know what happened."

He glanced back at the stone. "I do. That rock is covered in magic. I tried to stop you from touching it, but you beat me to it. What did you see? It's like you weren't even here anymore."

Swallowing hard, I could taste the bile burning my throat. "I don't think I was. I could see into Amelie's memories. She watched the wolves tear her parents apart."

Sebastian growled.

"I was about to see the wolves who took her until I was

thrust out. We need to see who they are." Clutching his hands, I pulled them away from my face and rushed to the stone. Before I could grab it, he tackled me to the floor, pinning my arms above my head. My body was too weak to even fight him off.

"Tyla, stop! I don't know what kind of magic this is. We don't know if it's good or bad."

I tried to move my arms and they wouldn't budge. "What does it matter if I can find out who took her? Whatever the reason for it being here is, it's obvious someone was meant to find it." Her journal still sat on the desk. "We need to read her journal."

Huffing, he loosened up his grasp and I still couldn't fight him off. "The stone made you weak. I'm barely holding you and you can't fight me."

My heart raced. I knew I was close to something; I just needed to get there. "Please, Sebastian. I don't know what's going on, but it feels right. You have to trust me." Jaw tense, he glared over at the stone and reached for it. "What are you doing?"

"I want to see what you saw." I held my breath and waited for him to touch it. He took a deep breath, and when he touched it . . . nothing happened. Brows furrowed, he held it in his hands and studied it. That was strange. He helped me to my feet and sat the stone on the desk. "I wonder why it's not working now," he said.

I reached over and scooped up the thick journal, flipping through the pages. There were entries from thirty years before, when we were in Finn's pack. "I don't know. Maybe it was only supposed to work one time." If so, we were screwed.

"I think we're done for the day," he suggested. "You can barely stand. I'll rent us a cabin out this way so we can come back tomorrow. We're obviously not going to get much more done today."

Nodding, I held the journal firmly in my grasp and picked up the stone, not expecting anything to happen. But that wasn't the case. I was sucked back into its magic. And this time, I may not have seen the three wolves who took Amelie, but I *did* see someone else.

TEN

SEBASTIAN

Tyla was still passed out by the time we got to the cabin I'd rented, so I carried her inside and laid her on the bed. Taking one last glance at her, I shut the door to the bedroom and retreated downstairs. I pulled out the stone and set it on the kitchen table. Why hadn't it worked for me?

Sliding my phone out, I dialed Seraphina's number. She was one of the Royal Pack elders, and a wolf who had the magic of a witch.

"Hello," she answered.

"Seraphina, it's Sebastian."

"Oh dear, you don't sound so good. I take it there's bad news."

Sighing, I sat down on the couch. "It's not good. In fact, I have to call Sophia and Erle as soon as I get off the phone with you."

"Where's Tyla?"

I closed my eyes and concentrated on her in the room above. She was still breathing heavily. "She's upstairs sleeping. We found her aunt and uncle ripped apart in the woods, with no sign of Amelie." She gasped. "But that's not what I'm calling about. Something else happened and I need your help. Have you ever encountered a blue stone with linking capabilities?"

"Like what exactly?" she asked.

"We found a smooth, blue stone on top of Amelie's journal. When Tyla touched it, she was thrust inside Amelie's memories. The downfall is that it drained Tyla's energy and completely wiped her out. That's why she's unconscious upstairs."

"What all did she see?"

"The first time she touched it, she could see her aunt and uncle's death. But then I stole the stone away because I thought it was hurting her."

"Did you see anything when you touched it?"

I picked up the stone and examined it. "No. I'm holding it now and it's not doing a goddamned thing."

"Interesting. And from what you said, I'm assuming she touched it more than once?"

"Yes, but I don't know what she saw the last time. She's not awake to tell me."

The line grew silent while I listened to Seraphina mumble to herself. Even she seemed to be puzzled. "Can you send me a picture of it?"

"Sure." I snapped a picture and sent it over. "You should have it now."

Seraphina cleared her throat and sighed. "It looks just like a normal moonstone. Granted, any kind of stone can hold magical capabilities, but it would take someone a lot more powerful than me to do a linking spell on it. My question is, why would anyone want to link Amelie's memories to it in the first place?"

"That's what I'm wondering. I don't get a bad vibe from the stone, but someone obviously wants this connection to Amelie. We just have to figure out who it is."

"And I have no doubt you'll figure it out. The only suggestion I have is to let Tyla get as much from the stone as she can. You might get the answers you're looking for."

I let out a humorless laugh. "I would if it didn't zap her energy. She's comatose right now and I have no clue how long it'll last."

"It's because she's not strong enough. If you were mated, like you *should* be, she'd have the energy of a royal."

"That's not likely to happen any time soon. She fights me every chance she gets."

She burst out laughing. "That comes from her mother. Just give her time."

I could feel the rage brewing just underneath my skin. "Unfortunately, time isn't on my side." We said our good-byes and I took a deep breath before answering the call that came through next. It was Tyla's parents. Her phone had been buzzing nonstop for the past two hours.

"Sophia," I greeted.

"Oh, thank God. What's going on? Where's Tyla?" she asked breathlessly.

"She's fine, just passed out at the moment. It's been a long day."

"Did you find Amelie? What about my sister? Is she okay?" Her desperation was evident.

I felt sick knowing the bomb I was about to drop on her. "Is Erle around?"

She sniffled. "Yes."

"Can you put me on speakerphone? I'd like to talk to you both." She did as I said and I could hear Erle in the background. "We didn't find Amelie, but we found signs that she was taken. Whoever did it used some very powerful magic. Thankfully, we might have some clues to help us."

"And my sister?" Sophia asked.

I held my breath and blew it out slow. "I'm so sorry, Sophia, but she didn't make it. Nor did Benjamin."

"What happened to them?" she demanded.

Erle huffed. "Soph, that's not something you need to know. Sebastian don't answer that."

Sophia burst out crying. "Why would anyone want to hurt them?"

"I think they were trying to help Amelie and got in the way. She was obviously the one the wolves wanted. I promise we'll find her. Tyla's not going to want to leave until we do."

"They were best friends," Erle said. "Attached at the hip, they were."

"And it'll be that way again when we find her. We'll bring her home."

Sophia sniffled again, but her voice was strong. "Sebastian?"

"Yes," I replied.

"Whatever happens, you bring my Tyla home safe. I don't care what you have to do, or who you have to leave behind, just make sure she gets back. I'm not going to let her kill herself over this mission. You both have so much to live for. I want to see her happy. I want grandbabies to hold."

I sighed. "Then talk some sense into her. She won't listen to me."

"She'll come around," she murmured. "Tyla's been through a lot of heartache. I know she'd kill me if I told you this, but she's just afraid. You need to show her she has nothing to worry about."

Leaning my head against the couch, I blew out a frustrated breath. Getting Tyla to listen was like trying to move a brick wall. I guess I was just going to have to break it down.

ELEVEN

TYLA

I could feel the warmth beside me and turned into it. Fingers caressed my arm and I smiled. Breathing deeply, Sebastian's scent filled my lungs and reality reared its ugly head. Gasping, I opened my eyes and sat up, head pounding. Sebastian stared back at me, the top half of his body bare. I really wanted to look under the covers to see if he was completely naked, but then I remembered why I was there in the first place. The memories from the stone flashed before my eyes.

"Where are we?" I asked.

Sebastian looked at me with his mesmerizing crystal blue eyes. "In a cabin just down the road from Amelie's. After you passed out last night, we needed a place to stay. I figured we could go back there today."

I looked at the clock and realized I'd been out for over twelve hours. "Holy shit, my parents. I need to call them."

Sebastian reached for my phone on the bedside table and tossed it to me. "It's already been done. I know you wanted to talk to them, but they kept calling. I had to tell them something."

My throat tightened and I nodded. It was probably best he'd done it anyway. "I understand. How did they take it?"

He shrugged. "Like I thought they would. They just want you home safe."

I glanced around the room for the stone. It was the only way I was going to find Amelie. "Where's the stone?" I asked.

"It's in safekeeping. What did you see this last time?"

Closing my eyes, I could see his face. He was a wolf, tall and very good looking with dark hair and hazel eyes. Amelie envisioned him a lot; they'd been intimate. "A man," I explained, opening my eyes. "He was Amelie's lover. She had to have mentioned him in her journal."

Nodding, he pulled the covers away and got out of bed. My eyes shot to his bare ass. I couldn't take my gaze away from his beautifully sculpted body. Sure, I was used to seeing the men in my pack naked, but I'd never get enough of Sebastian. He slid on a pair of pants and walked over to a table in the corner where the journal sat. He picked it up and tossed it to me.

"I didn't read any of it. I figured you'd want to be the one to do it," he murmured.

"Thanks," I said, holding it to my chest.

He nodded again and walked by me to grab his shirt. "I also talked to Seraphina. She said only someone really powerful can do the kind of linking spell found on that stone."

I opened the journal to a random page. "Maybe Amelie knows someone like that. I guess we'll find out." My stomach growled. "We should probably get something to eat soon." I hadn't eaten since we'd left Wyoming.

Sebastian put on his shirt and headed for the door. "As soon as you're ready, we'll go." He glanced back at me one more time before shutting the door behind him.

Looking down at my hands to find dirt still caked under my nails, I realized I desperately needed a shower. Once I was showered and dressed, I tucked the journal under my arm and met Sebastian downstairs.

"I'm ready," I called out. More snow had started to fall, and it'd do little to help us on our mission, covering up the tracks we'd followed the day before. I looked out the window and groaned. "What are we going to do?"

Sebastian followed my gaze. "Our best bet is to go through the journal today, front to back. And tomorrow, we can return to Amelie's."

Nodding, I fully agreed with him. It was going to take all day to get through her journal. Hopping in the car to get something to eat, I opened it up and started reading while Sebastian drove us around. I skimmed through the first entries from when we were kids. Thankfully, she didn't write in it every day or I'd never get through them all. She only wrote when she felt the need to let out her feelings.

GRADUATION

GRADUATION DAY! I'm so glad to be done with high school, but now comes the hard part. I have no clue what I want to do in life. Tyla wants to be a veterinarian and I know she'd be great at it, but what am I good at? I love plants and rare *gems. Maybe I should become a teacher and share my knowl-edge with young minds. All of the colleges I applied to have accepted me, but I haven't told anyone yet, especially Tyla. She wants to go away to college, and her parents can't afford to send her. I can't leave her behind. Maybe once she mates with Finn I'll go off on my own. Why not, right? Hopefully I'll meet a rugged wolf to sweep me off of my feet.*

My HEART HURT and I shut the journal, as Sebastian pulled us into the parking lot of a local mom and pop restaurant.

"Everything okay?" he asked.

Shaking my head, I glanced down at the journal. "Amelie lied to me."

"About what?"

I shrugged. "Nothing major. When we graduated high school, she knew my parents couldn't afford to send me to college, so she lied about not being accepted anywhere and stayed home. I can't believe she did that."

"That was her choice, Tyla."

"I know, but I didn't want her to put her life on hold because of me. Maybe our pack splitting up was good for her. She ended up going to college and getting a teaching degree."

"Why exactly did your pack split up?"

My stomach growled and I clutched it. "Do you mind if we talk about this later? I'm starving."

Pursing his lips, I knew he wasn't finished with me, but I wasn't ready to talk about it. That time would come soon enough.

I ate more than I'd ever eaten in my entire life and even brought back extra food. With everything going on, there was no telling when I'd get the chance to eat again. Sebastian stayed close and patrolled around the house sporadically as I read through the journal. His presence was a much needed comfort.

Skimming through the journal, I went through almost every entry for the past thirty years, looking for names I didn't recognize. Even during our time of separation, it was nice knowing she'd missed me as much as I'd missed her. At one point, I'd tried to get her to move to Wyoming, but she loved it in North Carolina. Now I could see why.

June 8

It was a good day today. I think I finally met the rugged wolf I've been waiting for. Jaret Bleddyn. He's just like me, a rogue. Don't get me wrong, the local pack has some pretty decent looking wolves, but this guy takes the cake. I met him out in the woods when I went searching for a plant to use in my next classroom demonstration. I have plans to see Jaret this weekend. I can't wait.

June 12

Tonight was my first date with Jaret. My parents weren't exactly thrilled about me going out with a lone wolf, but he's absolutely perfect. He drove us to Asheville and we went to the Biltmore House. It's strange, but every time he looks at me, I get this weak feeling in my knees. In fact, I'm so sure he's my mate, I gave in and slept with him. It was the most amazing night of my life. There was no way I could resist him.

"Tyla?" Sebastian called.

I waved my hand in the air. "Over here." Sitting up, I made room for him on the couch.

He sat beside me, dressed in only a pair of dress pants with the button undone. I was starting to think he didn't own a pair of jeans. "Any wolves out there?" I asked.

"Not that I can tell." My gaze drifted to the opening in his pants again and my pulse raced. A small smirk splayed across his lips. He knew I wanted him, and with each passing day, it was getting harder and harder to fight against my need. He tapped the journal, grabbing my attention. "Find anything?"

Sitting up straighter, I cleared my throat. "Actually, I did. She was involved with a wolf named Jaret Bleddyn. Looks like they were intimate."

His heart rate flared, along with his desire; serving only to fuel my mine more. Dammit, he was going to kill me. "Is that the last entry?" he asked.

I shook my head. I hadn't gotten all the way to the end. Flipping through the pages, I got to the last entry. It was dated just three weeks prior. I read it out loud.

"I DECIDED TO DO IT. Tonight is the full moon and I'm going to complete the bond with Jaret. He's on his way now to get me. My parents are angry. They say he's not my true mate. How can that be when I feel the way I do? Their constant badgering has left me no choice but to see him in secret. Why couldn't they just understand? The decision has been made and I'm going to see it through. Once they meet him, they'll see he's my mate. I love him."

SEBASTIAN'S GAZE NARROWED. "So your aunt and uncle never met the guy?"

Closing the journal, I sat it on the table and grabbed my phone. "Doesn't look like it. And Amelie had been seeing him for months by that point. It makes no sense." I dialed Blake's number and waited for him to pick up.

"What's up, Tyla?"

"Hey, Boss. You doing okay this morning?"

He chuckled. "Believe it or not, I can run my ranch on my own. You just happen to make it easier."

"Trust me, I wish I was there."

"Is everything all right?" he asked.

Blake didn't know I was a shifter and he probably never would. "Everything's great," I lied, "just visiting some of my family. Is there any way you can look up someone for me?" He was one of the best undercover cops in the country and his resources were vast.

"Sure, what's the name?"

"Jaret Bleddyn," I said, before spelling it out.

"All right, I'll see what I can do. I'll give you a call as soon as I find something."

"Thanks, Blake." We hung up and I blew out a frustrated breath. "If she's mated, Jaret has to be somewhere."

"Not unless the wolves killed him," Sebastian replied. The thought made my chest tighten.

"Let's hope not. I don't want Amelie going through that kind of heartache." My voice cracked and I wanted to kick myself in the ass for letting my emotions slip.

"You sound like you've been through it before."

Eyes burning, I couldn't stop the tears even if I wanted to. "I need some fresh air." I jumped to my feet and rushed outside. Snow fell from the sky and I lifted my face to it, the cold flakes melting on my warm cheeks. Gripping the wooden rail of the porch, I squeezed it, waiting for Sebastian to join me. When he did, I could feel his warmth beside me.

"I think it's time you told me the truth. You're pushing me away and I want to know why. I know you're scared; I can feel it. You don't have to be afraid of me."

His hand closed over mine and my heart ripped wide open.

"I'm not afraid of you, Sebastian. I'm afraid of being with you."

"Why?" He grabbed my wrist and turned me to face him. "Tell me."

My tears burned like hot lava down my cheeks. I couldn't keep him in the dark forever. "Have you ever lost someone you loved?" I asked.

He nodded. "A lot of them. My parents, family, some of my closest friends. I've been around a while."

Which was true, he was about fifty years older than me. "What about a person you were *in* love with?"

His jaw tensed. He knew where I was going with this. "No, but I take it you have. Was his name Cliff?"

My mouth gaped and I gasped. "How did you know that?"

He lowered his gaze to our clasped hands. "I followed you the other day and heard you talk to him."

"Looks like you have a habit of following me."

His head lifted, eyes flashing. "I'm an unmated male trying to keep my mate safe. Given our situation, it's the only thing that has helped. And also this," he said, squeezing my hands. "Your touch keeps me sane." He wasn't lying. I could feel his tension seeping away. "Was he human?" he asked.

I nodded. "Basically, our relationship was doomed from the start. No one knew I was dating a human. My parents, especially my mother, would've given me a hard time. But I loved Cliff. He was a good man."

"What happened?"

Closing my eyes, I remembered seeing his face for the last time in the hospital. I could still hear the last beats of his heart. "When I wasn't aging, I had to cut ties with him before he noticed. A few years later, I went to check on him and found out he was in the hospital, dying from cancer. Before he took his last breath, I was able to see him again."

Sebastian nodded in understanding. "So you're afraid of losing me? Is that it?" He moved closer and cupped my face in his hands. "I can promise you I'm not going anywhere."

I shook my head. "I'm cursed, Sebastian. Everyone I've ever loved has been taken from me." Taking a deep breath, I blew it out slowly. "You don't know this, but I was set to be mated to another man thirty years ago."

"Go on."

I didn't want to tell him about my intimacies with other men, but it was the only way to get him to understand. "He was our pack leader and one of my closest friends. We knew that to make our pack strong, our union was the best bet. He needed a strong female and I was the strongest. However, he wasn't the only one who wanted me."

Recollection sparked in his gaze. "Is that why your pack split up?"

"More like demolished. As far as I know, everyone was killed, except for a few of us."

"And your intended, what happened to him?"

I shrugged. "Killed. He said he would come for me and he never did. My pack was slaughtered because of me and I've never been able to forgive myself for it. Finn told me to run when I should've followed him and fought. I will never make that same mistake again."

He tilted my face up. "But you lived to see another day.

Things happen for a reason, love. Your choices brought you to me. This is where you belong."

My lip quivered and I bit it. "What if I lose you too? I can't bear the thought."

Before I could take a breath, he closed his lips over mine, wrapping his arms around my waist. I was too tired to fight, and gave in, opening myself up to him. His lips were warm, his hands rough as they reached underneath the hem of my shirt. I didn't want to let him go, but he broke away first.

Leaning his forehead to mine, he closed his eyes. "If you don't finish this, you will surely lose me. The rage will drive me insane and I won't be able to control it. You need to make the choice soon, your fear . . . or my life." He stepped away and disappeared inside, only to emerge again and take off into the woods.

I stood there frozen, with the weight of this words sinking in. He'd given me his terms and now it was my turn. Only, I didn't know what to do.

TWELVE

TYLA

For the rest of the night, Sebastian stayed in his wolf form and kept guard outside. I tried to search for the stone but couldn't find it. He had it hidden well. It wasn't until the early morning hours when I awoke to sounds of him coming inside and hopping in the shower. He was avoiding me. I guess I deserved it.

"Knock, knock," I said, tapping on the bathroom door. It opened slightly and steam billowed out.

"Yeah?" Sebastian replied.

I could see his form through the cloudy, glass shower door. I fought back the urge to say 'fuck my fears' and jump in the shower with him. When I didn't answer, he opened the door and looked at me.

"Can I help you?"

Clearing my throat, I turned my head. "Where's the stone?"

He shut the shower door. "Safe, why?"

"I want to use it. We need to know more."

Opening the door again, he turned the water off and got

out. I met his gaze and it took all I had to keep it there. "Let's go to Amelie's again and search around. If by the end of the day we don't find anything new, I'll let you use it. You don't want to be like the walking dead right now, it'll waste the rest of the day."

As much as I wanted to fight it, he had a point. Nodding, I stepped back. "Deal. I'll meet you downstairs."

While I waited for him, I heated up my leftover steak from the day before and saved half for him, putting it on a separate plate along with half of my baked potato.

He stopped at the door and lifted a brow. "What are you doing?"

My stomach growled. "If I'm hungry, I know you are too. You didn't eat anything last night, so I'm giving you half of my steak." When he sat down, I could tell a smile was just beneath the surface. I passed him a fork and he stuck it in the meat. "When we get back to Wyoming, I'll cook you a meal. I'm actually pretty good at it. So don't judge me by this chunk of reheated beef."

He ate a bite and smiled. "So I've heard. Everyone talks about your cooking. I'll admit, I was jealous when my brother told me you made him an apple pie."

I burst out laughing. "It was an apology for giving him a black eye. Don't let him make you think it's because he was special."

"I'll have to tell him that."

We ate the rest of our food and I was glad to finally see a smile on his face. "Are you going to help me look through the house, or patrol the perimeter?"

He got up and put his plate in the sink. "Both. I want to

see if there are any new tracks. Maybe even a sign from Jaret. We still don't know if they completed the bond."

"True. I didn't smell anyone other than my family in her house."

"Then they must've been meeting at his place," he said, opening the front door. "If only we could find it."

My phone rang and I quickly pulled it out of my pocket. "Blake, hey. Did you find anything on Jaret?"

He sighed and I knew it was going to be bad news. "Are you sure his name is Jaret Bleddyn?"

"Yes."

"Tyla, I can't find anything on this guy. There is no Jaret Bleddyn in any part of the world."

Sebastian heard and looked dumbfounded. "I don't know what to do," I whispered, more to myself than to anyone else.

"You're not in any trouble are you?" Blake asked.

"No, it's not like that. I'll be fine. I guess I just got his name wrong."

"And you're *sure* you're okay?"

"Yes." I laughed, hoping to appease him. The last thing I needed was for him to get involved with what we were doing.

He sighed. "All right. Call me if you need anything else."

"Will do." I hung up and slammed my phone down on the table. "Looks like we're back to square one. My cousin is involved with someone she doesn't even know."

We walked out to the car and Sebastian glanced at me from the other side. "We need to find out who he is, and fast. There's a reason he didn't want her to know who he was."

Amelie's house was almost completely cleaned up by the end of the day, but I couldn't find any more clues, other than a couple of pictures in her room of her and the mysterious Jaret Bleddyn. I was ready to head back to our cabin and try the stone. Surely, I'd have more luck with it.

Sebastian had been patrolling the grounds for the past couple of hours, searching for tracks. If he'd found something, he would have been back long ago. The sound of footsteps scraped across the wooden porch and I rushed downstairs.

"Did you find anything?" I asked, turning the corner into the living room.

The man in front of me wasn't Sebastian. He was a wolf, yet I couldn't smell him. Tall, with dark green eyes and long, brown hair, the guy was dressed in dirty jeans and a plaid button down shirt. His eyes flashed when he saw me. "Well, well, well. What do we have here?"

He walked forward and I took a step back. "Who are you?" When I took another step back, a set of arms snatched me from behind. "Let me go." I growled and bucked. My nails lengthened and I dug them in his arms, ripping his flesh.

He yelled and let me go, but not before smacking me across the cheek. It burned, but I stood strong and faced him. This guy had short, brown hair and glowing gray eyes. His fangs grew in length, and so did his claws.

I glared straight at him. "You don't scare me, you worthless pile of dog shit."

The long haired wolf burst out laughing. "We got a feisty one on our hands."

"Where's Amelie?" I commanded.

He smiled wide. "You talking about the busty blonde who lived here?"

"Where is she?" I shouted as loud as I could. Sebastian was sure to hear me now.

Long hair shrugged. "Somewhere up north. We were instructed to kill whoever came looking for her. But I don't think that'll be the case with you; at least, not yet. I wanna have a little fun with that body of yours first."

My eyes flashed and I was ready to shift. "You can try."

The guy behind me tried to grab me again, but I dropped to the floor and punched him in the balls. As he went down, I jumped over him and out the front door. I didn't get far before Long Hair lunged and grabbed me around the waist, bringing me down on the gravel driveway.

The breath was knocked out of my lungs and I gasped, choking for air.

"That wasn't so hard." He laughed maliciously. "I thought you'd put up more of a fight."

Sebastian's rage unleashed and I could feel his anger. "I don't have to," I said, sucking in a breath.

The loudest growl I'd ever heard echoed through the trees. Long Hair backed away from me and shifted, ready to fight. The other guy stumbled out of the house and joined him, both massive gray wolves. Sebastian didn't waste any time in his attack. Long Hair lunged for him and they toppled over one another. Short Hair turned and glared at me.

"Mad that I kicked those tiny things between your legs?" I growled. Ripping off my clothes, I felt the magic of the shift shimmer across my body. He roared and lunged at me just as I shifted, but I dodged out of his reach. I was prepared to fight, but Sebastian had already beaten me to it.

Tearing the wolf open with one swipe of his paw, Sebastian sent his blood splattering across the ground. The howls of pain were deafening. I stood back and watched the carnage unfold before me. Sebastian was lethal, tearing both wolves apart limb from limb. The rage had consumed him and it scared the hell out of me. He didn't slow in his attack, even when they were clearly dead.

Shifting back, I took a step forward. "Sebastian, stop," I said low.

His gaze lifted, eyes still glowing. He growled and I held my breath. He wouldn't hurt me, but seeing him like that terrified me. Blood dripped from his mouth as he stalked toward me. I stepped back and lost my footing, falling on my backside. He towered over me, his fangs scraping along my neck.

"It's okay," I whispered. "Come back to me." He backed up quickly, eyes darting back and forth from the dead wolves to me. "Sebastian, please shift back."

Instead of shifting, he darted off into the woods. He could smell my fear.

As fast as I could, I threw on my clothes and ran inside to grab the keys. If there were more wolves around, they'd find the carnage. I didn't want to be there if that happened. Grabbing his clothes on the way out, I jumped in the car and raced out of the driveway.

Back at our cabin, I could sense Sebastian was near. His torment was thick in the air. I had to find him.

Shifting back into my wolf form, I took off into the forest and followed his scent. Thankfully, he wasn't hiding it from me. Coming to a stop at a lake that was partially frozen over, I waited as Sebastian rolled around in the water. When he was done, he traipsed out and shook off his fur, no longer covered in blood.

I approached him slowly and he never took his gaze off of mine. Rubbing my head under his chin, a satisfied growl rumbled in his chest. I just wanted him to come back to me. I nudged him with my nose and licked the side of his neck, only to come away with the taste of blood in my mouth. My mind whirled and a flood of emotions exploded inside of me. *What the hell did I just do?*

His feelings became my own and I could see everything inside of his mind. The pain became too much and I screamed as I shifted back, clutching the sides of my head. I closed my eyes and fell to the ground, hoping it would stop.

Usually when you tasted a mate's blood, a vision of your future would occur, but there was only pain, hatred, and rage.

"Tyla!" Sebastian pulled me into his arms and held me tight. "Tyla, what's wrong?" He grabbed my hands and jerked them away from my face.

I looked into his eyes, and realized what he'd been keeping from me this whole time. *"Sebastian, it's too much,"* I thought to him, knowing he'd hear me in his mind.

Eyes wide, he shook his head and shut me out. The relief was instant, but his agony was just below the surface. It wouldn't stay hidden for long. "Dammit, Tyla, you weren't supposed to see all of that." Lifting me up, he carried me back to the house.

My eyes burned. "I didn't realize it was that bad." And all because of me. To top it all off, I hadn't received a vision of our future. That could only mean one thing . . . death.

THIRTEEN

TYLA

I wanted to talk to Sebastian about what had happened, but he was struggling to keep it together. He sat on the couch, watching TV like nothing was wrong, but I knew the truth. He thought he was shutting me out, but I could still see his thoughts. He had seen me get slapped across the cheek and that vision was on loop in his mind. He blamed himself for not getting there fast enough.

Sneaking away, I tiptoed upstairs to the bedroom and dialed Bailey's number. She knew Sebastian better than anyone.

"Tyla, oh my God," she said, forgoing the usual greeting. "What's going on? I heard about your family. I'm so sorry."

"And it gets worse. We were attacked today. It appears there's more to this whole story that we haven't figured out yet."

"Do you need help? We can send others out there to you."

Sighing, I sat down on the bed. "The more of us around,

the more attention it'll bring. And unfortunately, we have another problem."

"What?"

Closing my eyes, I concentrated on Sebastian's mind. He was afraid I was scared of him after seeing him today. My heart broke. "Sebastian's a lot worse than I thought. I accidentally drank some of his blood today."

"Did the link open up?" she asked.

"It did. And what I saw terrified me," I whispered. "There wasn't a vision either. I just *knew* there'd be no happy ending for us."

"You don't know that. The visions could be tainted because of his rage. Besides, the future always changes with the decisions we make." She blew out a sigh. "What else happened?"

"He not only killed the wolves who attacked us, he shredded them apart. I've never seen him like that before. His mind is in a dark place, Bailey. He's trying to keep me out, but it's not working. It's taking him over."

"What are you going to do? Please don't make him suffer. I love him and I know you do too."

My eyes burned as Sebastian's words echoed in my mind, "If you don't finish this, you will surely lose me. The rage will drive me insane and I won't be able to control it. You need to make the choice, your fear . . . or my life."

"Tyla, you there?" Bailey said desperately.

I blew out a shaky breath. "I know what to do."

"You do?"

"Yep. I'll call you soon." I hung up and started for the door, heart racing. Sebastian was still on the couch with an arm draped over his eyes. His breathing was heavy, but he wasn't asleep. He was fighting his demons, visions of red flashing through his mind. I tiptoed over and watched him, wondering if he was going to acknowledge me.

"I know you're there." His voice was low and dark.

Biting my lip, I took a step forward. Slipping my pants and underwear down my legs as quietly as I could, I closed the distance. When I ran my hands up his thighs, his body jumped at the contact and then relaxed, mind clearing for a brief second.

"What are you doing?" he murmured.

Climbing up on his lap, I straddled his waist. "A little bit of this," I said, sliding his hand up my shirt. "And a little bit of that . . ." I ran my hand over the zipper of his jeans and rubbed his arousal. He sucked in a breath and dropped his arm, eyes blazing.

"Don't start something you can't finish," he warned.

I knew what I was getting myself into. I couldn't let him suffer any longer, not when I could see what he was going through. His pain was now my pain. I leaned down and kissed him, biting his lip between my teeth. "I guess it's a good thing I plan on finishing then."

His grip tightened and he closed his lips over mine. I could barely breathe, but I knew he needed it. His erection pressed into me and he rocked me against it, his fingers digging into my hips.

"I need you so fucking bad," he growled, sliding his lips down my neck. Fisting his hands in my shirt, he ripped it apart and tossed it on the floor, groaning when he sucked a nipple between his teeth.

I gasped and leaned my head back, my whole body trembling from his touch. I needed him inside of me. Sliding my hands down his smooth, bare chest, I stopped at his pants and freed him. He lifted me up and kicked his pants to the floor before setting me back down. Moaning, I rubbed my wetness all over him, loving the way he growled deep in his chest at my movements. Raising my hips, I slid down onto him inch by inch, until he was all the way in. He filled me completely, stretching me to the point of pain.

Gripping the back of my neck, Sebastian pulled me to him, ravishing me with his lips. "You have no idea how long I've waited for this."

I slid up and down his length, the delicious ache sending tremors throughout my body. The connection between us opened, and instead of seeing red, I saw visions of me, laughing and smiling—Sebastian's memories of me. I could feel his need to protect me and how hard it was for him not to force his claim on me.

Holding him tight, I rode him as hard as I could, loving the sound of his groans. I was so close to the edge. His teeth grazed along my neck, but I grasped his face, drawing him to my lips. "I'm not ready for that," I whispered breathlessly.

Eyes flashing, he drew his fangs back. "I need to feel all of you, love."

I kissed him again. "You will. Just give me a little more time."

Gripping a handful of my hair, he held me to his lips and pushed his body up into me hard. My whole body tightened around him and I let go, screaming out my release. He grunted and gripped the side of my hip, holding me down as he came inside me. I leaned forward, resting my forehead to his and smiled. He was happy; I could feel it and see it in his mind.

Wrapping his arms around my waist, he lifted me up and stood.

"What are you doing?" I asked.

His eyes bored into mine and I shivered. "Taking you to bed. I'm not done with you yet."

I could barely move the next morning, as the entire night before was spent in an orgasmic haze. Sebastian hadn't been kidding when he'd said he wasn't done with me. His scent was all over the sheets, but when I reached for him, he wasn't there. Opening my eyes, I sat up and listened. His mind was shut off from me, but I could hear him outside on the porch, tapping a finger on the wooden railing.

Sliding out of bed, I grabbed a blanket and wrapped it around my body. When I got downstairs, I saw him outside on the deck, bare-chested, wearing only a pair of pants. The snow fell all around him, his whitish-blond hair covered in flakes. Something was wrong; I could feel it. It was almost like the awkwardness after a one night stand, only I'd never had one of those to compare. Taking a deep breath, I opened the door and stepped out. He didn't move.

"Sebastian?"

He glanced over his shoulder. "Good morning, love."

"What's wrong?" I walked up and stood beside him, my shoulder brushing his skin.

He leaned over the railing on his elbows and looked at me. "Why didn't you want me to taste your blood last night? Are you afraid of me getting in your head?"

Averting my gaze, I focused on the woods, ashamed of my fears. "The last thing you need to worry about are my insecurities, especially while you're battling your own issues. It's not fair."

"That's not it, Tyla. There's something else. What is it?"

Blowing out a sigh, I turned to face him, his piercing blue eyes seeing right through me. "When I took your blood yesterday, there wasn't a vision. From what I've heard, you're supposed to see visions of a glorious future together after the first exchange. I didn't get that."

His jaw tensed. "What did you see?"

"Blood, darkness, pain. Bailey says it could've been your thoughts overpowering the moment, but I don't know. Having you, then losing you, would kill me. I'm afraid of what I'll see when you take my blood."

My eyes burned, and I tried and failed at blinking back the tears. Sebastian pulled me into his arms, my face resting against his chest. His strong heartbeat was music to my ears. "Don't you think I'm scared too?"

"Of what?" I asked.

He pulled back and cupped my face in his hands. "We don't know if it's me hindering our visions, or if it's our true future. Whatever happens, it doesn't necessarily mean it's you losing me. What if I'm the one who loses you? As your mate and protector, I don't want to fail."

"You won't. It's not in your blood."

A sad smile spread across his lips. "But I would rather die knowing I had a few happy moments with you, than nothing at all. You have no idea how much last night helped me."

I placed my hands over his and smiled as the blanket slid down my body. "It helped me too." Leaning up on my toes, I pressed my lips to his. Our future was unknown, but he had a point. I'd rather have a few happy moments with him than nothing at all.

"The full moon is coming soon." His hands cupped my backside, holding me against the bulge in his pants. "I want to complete the bond."

I stared up at him, completely at a loss for words. He tucked a strand of hair behind my ear, eyes searching mine. I wanted to do it, but it was all happening so fast. Before I could answer, his eyes flashed and he growled, his attention snapping to the woods.

"Sebastian, what's wrong?"

He pulled me behind him, his body tense. Then I realized what was going on; a wolf was in the distance. "Go inside, Tyla," he commanded. I did as he said and raced upstairs, throwing on a T-shirt and pants before rushing back down. Eyes closed, Sebastian stood by the door. "He's getting closer."

All I could sense was one wolf, but it could be a trap. I couldn't let him go out there alone. He took off his pants and opened the door. I started to follow him, but he held out his arm. "You're not coming with me, Tyla."

Jaw clenched, I stood up to him, daring him to try and make me stay. "You may be an alpha, but so am I. If you want me to be your mate, you have to let me be one. That means protecting you as well. Let me go out there and draw this wolf in while you shield your presence. When he gets close you can attack." I rested my hand against his cheek. "We fight together."

He huffed and nodded at the door. "Go, before I change my mind." Instead of shifting, I jumped off the deck and took off for the woods. Sebastian caught up to me after shifting. He was beautiful, and a hell of a lot larger than me in my wolf form. I watched him run off into the woods and disappear.

The other wolf was close, maybe a mile out. A small clearing was up ahead and I stopped in the middle of it. Whatever happened, I'd be ready.

"I'm okay," I said, hoping Sebastian could hear me in his mind. It was going to take some getting used to knowing I could speak to him without actually talking. The only problem was, I couldn't hear him back. He had to take my blood in order for the link to be open both ways.

The other wolf picked up his speed and my heart raced; he sensed me. By the sound of his paws on the ground, he was in wolf form. I thought about shifting, but when the massive gray wolf finally came into view and stopped at the edge of the clearing, I froze. Sucking in a breath, I stared into a set of golden, amber eyes.

"This can't be," I whispered, closing a hand over my mouth. He charged toward me, and me to him. I had to touch him to make sure he was real. He even had the same patch of white fur between his eyes. We were about to close the distance when a white blur caught my eye.

"No!" I screamed, holding out my hand. Sebastian lunged in the air, ready to strike. I raced toward him and jumped on his back, wrapping my arms around his neck. "Sebastian, no!"

Growling, he was pulled off course until my hold slipped. I rolled across the ground and yelped when the edge of a stick punctured a hole in my left shoulder. Pain shot through my body as I tried desperately to pull the stick out, but I couldn't reach it.

"Tyla!"

The stick was pulled out and I was lifted off the ground, only it wasn't Sebastian holding me . . . it was Finn. He looked in my eyes and I in his. It was really him. "Finn," I breathed, his face growing blurry from my tears. His brown hair was a little longer on top, but other than that he looked the same. For thirty years I'd thought he was dead, and now, he was standing before me. I touched his face and smiled. "You're alive."

"Come on, let's get you out of here."

He turned to leave the clearing and my mind exploded with nothing but red. Sebastian stood in human form, blocking our path—his murderous glare set on Finn. I hissed in pain, his raging emotions blasting my mind. It only got worse when he saw the blood dripping down my shoulders. He blamed himself for the wound. "Get your hands off her now or I'll rip your head off your fucking body."

Finn held me tighter. "I'd like to see you try."

"Stop!" I shouted. I glanced up at Finn and sighed. "Put me down. He's not your enemy."

He glared at Sebastian and back at me. "But you're hurt. We need to take care of that shoulder."

"I'll be fine. Now set me down, please." He did as I said and I hissed in pain.

Sebastian hurried over and swiped my hair away from the wound so he could take a look. "Fuck," he growled. "Why did you jump in my way?"

Swallowing hard, I looked over at Finn. "I couldn't let you hurt him. He's a friend from my past."

Finn scoffed. "I was much more than a *friend*, Tyla."

Sebastian tensed and faced him, stepping in front of me. "I don't care who you are, that was in the past. I'm her true mate."

Finn's gaze narrowed. "And I'm her first mate. Looks like we're going to have a problem."

FOURTEEN

W hen we got back to the house, I entered first, with both guys following behind me. There were clean towels in the laundry room, so I grabbed one and tossed it to Finn. "I'll be right back." He wrapped the towel around his waist and paced the living room floor while I retreated upstairs. Sebastian joined me and ripped off my shirt so I wouldn't have to lift my shoulders. "I'm seriously going to have to go shopping. This is the second shirt you've ripped."

His fingers gently traced over my wound. "I didn't enjoy ripping this one, love. The last thing I wanted was for you to get hurt." He moved me over to the bed and I sat down.

"It's not your fault. I didn't know it was going to be Finn."

"He's the alpha you spoke of, isn't he?" I nodded and hissed when he touched my wound again. "Were you lovers?"

Sighing, I nodded again. "It was a long time ago, Sebastian."

"It doesn't matter. You loved him. Just the *thought* of you being with him makes me so goddamned furious I can barely see straight." The smell of his blood unexpectedly permeated the room and I felt its warmth drip onto my wound.

"What are you doing?" I asked, before I realized the answer. The pain subsided and I could feel the flesh mending back together. He kissed my shoulder and smoothed a hand over it.

"My blood can heal you. It's one of the benefits of being true mates." I'd known that, but never thought it would work so quickly.

I turned around and kissed him. He saw Finn as a threat and I could feel it. He needed to know there was nothing to worry about. "I know you're my mate, Sebastian, and he's not going to take me away from you. But, I need to know what happened over the last thirty years. In order to do that, I have to talk to him. You need to let me go to him."

Jaw tense, he cursed under his breath. "You better hope he doesn't try to take you away from me. If he does, I won't hesitate in ripping him apart. That I can promise."

I nodded. "I just need answers, nothing more." He moved out of the way so I could grab another T-shirt from my bag. It didn't even hurt when I lifted my shoulders to put it on. Before walking out the door, I glanced over my shoulder. *"Thank you."*

He lifted his gaze and nodded.

Hurrying downstairs, I found Finn standing just outside. As I stepped out of the door, he scooped me into his arms.

"When I caught your scent in the woods, I thought I was in a fucking dream. I never thought I'd see you again."

Tears spilled down my cheeks. "I thought you were dead. Why didn't you come for me?"

He pulled back, eyes wide. "I had been, until Sarah and Benjamin told me you never made it out alive."

Gasping, I clutched a hand to my chest. "Why would they tell you that? They knew I was alive. Did Amelie tell you that as well?"

He shook his head. "I haven't seen her since the attack. I passed through this way many years ago on my search for you and found Sarah and Benjamin. That's when they told me."

I felt sick, betrayed. Why the hell would they do that? "What about the rest of our pack? What happened to them?"

Sighing, he grabbed my hands and squeezed. "There are some who still follow me, but over the years, most have turned up dead or missing. So when I was passing through and smelled the dead wolves at Amelie's, I knew something was wrong. That's when I went searching through the woods and found you."

"Why are our people showing up dead?"

He huffed. "I don't know. That's why I wanted to check on your family, to make sure they were okay."

"Amelie's gone, we believe she's been kidnapped. That's why we're here. She called and said she needed help. When we showed up, she was missing and we found my aunt and uncle dead in the woods. I don't know who took her." Then I thought of Jaret. "Do you know of a wolf named Jaret Bleddyn?"

He shook his head. "Doesn't sound familiar, why?"

I shrugged. "I think Amelie's mated to him. I had a cop friend search for him, but the name doesn't show up anywhere."

"Have you found anything else that could help?" he asked.

I glanced back into the house, where I knew the stone was hidden. "There is one way, but it doesn't come without a price." I faced him again. "We found a moonstone on Amelie's journal. When I touch it, it thrusts me into her memories. But when I use it for a long period of time, it zaps my energy. If we were attacked, I'd be too vulnerable."

"Fuck," he grumbled. "I don't like the sound of this. You're not safe here."

"I know. We've already been attacked once. Those are the wolves you found at Amelie's. They'd said they were instructed to kill anyone who showed up over there. I don't know what that means."

Letting my hands go, he ran them angrily through his hair. "I don't either, but I'm going to help. We'll find Amelie and bring our pack together."

My heart hurt at hearing his words. I wasn't a part of his pack anymore. He pulled me into his arms and I pulled out of his embrace.

"Sorry, baby. I didn't mean to hurt you."

"You didn't hurt me. It's just . . . he's my mate now," I murmured.

"You were supposed to be mine."

"I know, and it would've been a mistake." It hurt to say it, but it was the truth.

"But you're not mated yet. Why?"

The thought made me smile. For the longest time, I'd thought I was cursed. Everyone I'd loved died on me, or at least I thought they had. Finn was alive and well. "I didn't want to lose him like I'd lost you. I never got over it, Finn. I loved you then, and I always will. But I'm not a part of your pack anymore. I haven't been for a long time. If you don't want to help me find Amelie, that's fine. I'll understand."

He grabbed my hand and kissed it. "You may not be mine anymore, but you will always be a part of my pack. I'll be back in a couple of days with the others. They'll be happy to know you're alive." Tearing the towel away, he handed it to me and smiled. "You sure he's your mate?"

"Oh, get out of here with that." I rolled my eyes and smacked his shoulder. "Sebastian's already on edge as it is, we don't need him coming down here to kill you. I've seen in his mind and it's not good. You being here only makes it worse."

He nodded. "I understand. But he needs to know I'm here to help. You and Amelie were a part of my pack. That's not something I'll just forget."

"He'll understand," I said, hoping I sounded convincing.

Finn glanced inside the house, then back to me. "Somehow, I'm not sure I believe that. I'll see you later." He gave me his phone number, then shifted into his wolf, taking off into the woods.

When I got inside, I called for Sebastian, but he was shielding himself from me. "Sebastian?"

I headed upstairs and went straight to the bathroom when I heard the shower running. The door was partially open and steam billowed out. I took off my clothes quickly and snuck inside. The shower doors were steamy and when I opened them, I expected to see Sebastian in there, but it was empty.

A chuckle came from behind just as I was pushed under the running water. "Hey! That's not funny." I pouted, turning in Sebastian's arm to playfully pinch his nipple.

He closed his lips over mine, pressing his body tightly against me. Trailing his mouth down my neck to my breasts, he bit my nipple and looked up at me. "I had to get his scent off of you."

"You have nothing to worry about."

"I know. I heard you talking to him. But that doesn't mean he won't still be a problem."

"He won't. He knows you're my mate. You have to trust me."

Grabbing my legs, he lifted me up, wrapping them around his waist. "I do trust you."

"Even without taking my blood?"

He backed me into the wall and circled his hips, sliding his cock against my center. "Yes, love. As much as I want to feel you completely, I can trust you without it."

With Finn back from the dead, my fears were squashed. I didn't really have a reason to hide from him. Leaning my head to the side, I brushed my hair away from my neck. "You don't have to go without it anymore," I replied.

Sebastian froze. "What are you saying?"

I clutched his face in my grasp. "I'm ready, Sebastian. Don't get me wrong, I'm afraid of the visions, or lack thereof, but I know we need to do this. I'm ready. I want you completely."

His eyes shifted and I watched as his fangs lengthened.

He leaned down and ran his tongue along my neck before sinking his teeth into my skin. The bite felt orgasmic, and that was when the vision started. Flashes of light, and glimmers of Sebastian laughing, played through my mind. It happened all too quickly and then it was gone. Once we were sucked back into the here and now, Sebastian pulled back, his eyes and teeth shifting to normal.

"Did you see that?" he asked.

I didn't know if what I saw had been good or bad. From what I gathered, our future was still undecided. "At least it wasn't visions of red," I said.

He chuckled. "I know it wasn't what you were hoping for, but it's a start. We'll make our own fate, together."

"Together," I agreed silently.

Pulling my lip in between his teeth, he kept his heated gaze on mine and sucked it. *"I hope you're ready for this."*

I dug my nails in his back and smiled. *"You have no idea."*

FIFTEEN

TYLA

"Hungry much?" Sebastian teased.

"Famished," I answered, chewing the last bite of my chicken. After our tryst in the shower, we'd gotten dressed and driven to the closest store to pick up some groceries. We'd also wanted to go into town to see if we could spot other wolves. No such luck there.

It felt wrong to be enjoying this time with him while my cousin was being held against her will, but Sebastian wanted me to eat before I used the stone. We both knew I needed as much energy as possible, in order to hold onto Amelie's memories as long as I could.

Grabbing my plate, he put it in the sink and sighed. "You ready to use the stone?"

He wasn't happy with me using it, but we didn't have a choice. Walking back over, he set the smooth, blue stone on the table and took the seat beside me. I couldn't tear my gaze away from it. It was as if it called to me somehow.

"I'm ready, but there's something that's been bothering me." He already knew because he could see it in my mind.

"Why don't you call your parents and ask them? You haven't talked to them since we left anyway. I bet they've called over a hundred times now."

He had a point. Dialing my parents' number, I waited for them to pick up. My mother was the one to answer, her voice a high-pitched shriek.

"You sure do know how to scare your mother to death!"

"Hello to you too, Mother," I said.

"What's going on? Have you found Amelie?"

Sebastian held my hand and squeezed. "No, we haven't, but I did find someone else."

"Who?"

"Finn." I waited for a gasp of excitement, or any kind of reaction for that matter, but it didn't come. Her silence confirmed my suspicion. "You knew he was alive . . ."

"Honey, I know what you're thinking—"

"Save it," I snapped.

She sighed, her voice sounding defeated. "What did he say?"

"You're not even going to deny it?"

"There's no point. I'm sorry for not telling you, but it was for the best. He would've found you and you'd be stuck mated to him. Where would that have left Sebastian?"

I didn't want to think about that. Sebastian nodded in agreement, but it still didn't change the fact she'd lied to me. And it hadn't been just my life she'd messed with. "It wasn't fair, Momma. Finn's been carrying around the guilt of my death for thirty years. When did you find out he was alive?"

"About ten years after the attack. That's when he found Sarah and Benjamin."

"Apparently, several people from our pack have been

found as well. Finn says they've been showing up dead over the years."

She gasped. "Oh no. Does he know who's killing them?"

"No. Make sure to tell Ryker what's going on so the pack can be on alert. He doesn't need to let any strange wolves close to you."

The line went quiet, but I could hear her breathing. Her past actions might have been for the best, but it didn't hurt any less. "Tyla, dear?"

Sebastian rubbed a hand down my back, soothing me. "I'm here," I said.

"I'm sorry for lying to you. You have to know it broke my heart to see you suffer, but I was only trying to protect you. If I had to do it all over again, I wouldn't change a thing. This path led you to Sebastian. It's the way it's supposed to be."

"I know."

"Why don't you just come home? If you can't find Amelie, there's nothing more you can do out there. I don't want you risking your life over this."

My gaze caught the stone. "I think I have a way to find her. If it doesn't work, we'll come home."

"Just be safe. I love you, honey."

"Love you too." I hung up and laid my head on the table.

"Were you serious about going home if we can't find her?" Sebastian asked.

"I'm hoping that's not the case," I said, turning to face him. "We *have* to find her. I can't imagine what's being done to her right now. And when I look through the stone, it's like I'm actually inside her body. I'm afraid of what I'm going to see this time around. If someone's hurting her, there's not a goddamned thing I can do."

He grabbed the stone and helped me to my feet. "At least now you don't have to see it alone. With our connection, I should be able to see it with you. Maybe I'll be able to help."

I hadn't even thought of that. "Let's get to it." I walked over to the couch and sat down. Taking a deep breath, I made sure my mind was completely open. Sebastian held out the stone and I took it, the memories flooding in.

SIXTEEN

SEBASTIAN

Tyla was still passed out, sleeping soundly in the bed. Her blonde curls fanned out over her pillow and on her face was a half-smile. She was so beautiful. It was late morning, and I could already feel the pull of the full moon drawing me to her. If she decided not to complete the bond tonight, I didn't know what I was going to do. I'd never wanted anything more in my life.

Waiting for her to awake, I sat and thought about all of the details we'd seen while she'd held the stone. Judging by the memories, Amelie was being kept in a dark basement with cement walls. In the vision, we were able to see a clock in the corner of the room with the same time as when we touched the stone. It was too convenient to be a coincidence. It wasn't long after that when it grew dark, interspersed with flashes of memories here and there. We realized then she had to be sleeping; there was a hazy shimmer around the visions.

Luckily, Amelie dreamt of Jaret. He looked familiar somehow, but I couldn't recall where I'd known him from.

I'd met thousands of wolves in my time, some in friendship and even more in battle. I couldn't place him. In Amelie's memory, they were sitting in a white gazebo by a small pond. There was a building in the background—apartments from what I could tell—with white siding and a green tin roof. That was what I was researching now. There had to be a place like that close by.

Tyla stirred and opened her eyes. She stretched, poking her breasts up in the air, making something stir down below. She was going to kill me.

"Good morning, love."

She turned to me and smiled. "Good morning to you too. What are you doing?"

I held up my phone. "Looking for buildings like the one we saw in Amelie's mind. It has to be somewhere near here. Maybe we can finally find this Jaret."

Groaning, she covered her face with a pillow. "God, I hope he's not dead. I don't want to find her only to tell her that her mate is gone."

"He very well could be. He hasn't even shown up at her house to check on her. If this was you, I'd be doing everything I could to find you. What's strange though, is I think I've met the guy before. He looks familiar."

"Really? That's weird. Maybe he just looks like someone you know."

I shrugged. "Maybe."

"Do you think he's not her true mate?" she asked.

"I don't know, but we'll see." I tapped on another apartment link and grinned from ear to ear. "Got it."

Tyla jumped out of bed and I showed it to her. Her eyes lit up. "You're right, that's it. Where's it at?"

I clicked on the directions and a map appeared. "Thirty minutes away." She rushed to get dressed and I couldn't help but watch her bounce around. After months of nothing but torture, she was finally mine. Shaking her head, she burst out laughing. "What's so funny?" I asked.

"Torture? Really?" She zipped up her jeans and waltzed over, grabbing my shoulders as she straddled my lap.

I cupped her ass and squeezed. "It *was* torture, just like you're doing to me now." My cock ached from her rubbing against it. I wanted nothing more than to tear into her, but we couldn't, and she knew it. "We have to go," I told her.

She nodded. "I know. I'm just ready to figure all this shit out so we can go home."

"You're not the only one." I smacked her ass and she got up to finish getting dressed. Once she was ready, we were on our way out the door.

"What do you think we'll find when we get there?" she asked.

My first thought was Jaret's dead body, but I had to stay positive. "Don't know. I guess we'll find out."

The drive didn't take long and when we pulled in, I didn't sense any other wolves around. But with the magic they were using, who knew anymore. They could be there and we wouldn't know it. I parked the car and we both got out.

"Our best bet is to walk around and see if we can catch Amelie's scent," I suggested.

Tyla slung her purse over her shoulder and grabbed my hand. "Let's go."

The building wasn't tall, but it was three levels and

spanned five acres. I couldn't find Amelie's scent on the first or second levels. However, when we got to the top, I picked it up.

"We're close. Her scent is faint, but it's there. Two doors down." Tyla took off for the door and looked in the apartment window. There were no curtains barring us from seeing inside, but it was empty—a dead end.

"I got his scent too, but it's faint, just like Amelie's."

Tyla's eyes went wide. "I can barely scent her. Must be nice to be a royal."

"You'll be one soon," I thought.

A small smile splayed across her lips. "How long do you think the place has been empty?"

"Two weeks, maybe?"

"I don't get it. It's like everything is being erased just to fuck with us," she griped. I could feel her frustration and the desperation to get her cousin back.

Putting my arm around her, I pulled her into my side. "It's standard procedure to clean the carpets and paint the walls before another tenant moves in, love. We just didn't know in time."

"Why do you think Jaret moved?"

"There are an infinite possibilities of reasons why he left." An idea sparked in my mind. Grabbing her hand, I pulled her down the hallway.

"What are you doing?"

"I have an idea."

"You are absolutely brilliant," Tyla gushed.

Smiling, I tucked a strand of her hair behind her ear. "I'm willing to try anything."

We'd grabbed a bite to eat while we waited on the apartment manager to give us a tour of the place. The snow had started to fall again, but we sat outside by the pond. There were others who pulled in and looked at us like we were crazy, sitting outside with no jackets on, but the cold didn't bother us. I could lie down in a bed of snow and never get frostbite. It was one of the many joys of being an Arctic wolf. I missed being in the icy regions of Canada where I was born. One day, I'd take Tyla there so she could see where I came from.

"Why didn't you tell me you missed home?" she asked.

I chuckled. "Prying in my mind again?"

She nudged me in the side. "Just looking out for you.

But I'd love to go to Canada some day. I've never been up that way."

"You'd love it. I still own a bunch of property up there. My parents left it all to me and my brothers."

"Wow. I guess all your money came from them then? You haven't had a job since you moved to Wyoming."

"How do you know?" I asked, watching her blush. "Were you watching me?"

She rolled her eyes. "Don't flatter yourself. I'll admit I was curious, and may have asked around."

"Why didn't you ask me? We were friends."

She shrugged. "I guess I didn't want you to know I was interested. Didn't think you'd care."

"That's what you get for assuming. Now what do you want to know? You can ask me anything."

She giggled. "You probably shouldn't have said that. I might take you up on it. But in all seriousness, where does your money come from? If I'm going to be your mate, I need to know this stuff."

"You do, huh? You're not going to take it all and run are you?"

"Depends on how much you got." She laughed. Her gray eyes twinkled, making me smile.

"I've lived a long time, Tyla. And so had my parents. I'm not going to lie, they did leave me with a fortune, but that's because they were around for over three hundred years. However, I do have my own money as well."

"What did you do?"

Grinning, I thought back to when I was a boy. "My first job was ice fishing. I went out there with my dad every morning. Since the cold didn't bother us, we were able to withstand the freezing temperatures all day long. We kept some of the fish we caught, but sold the rest to the local markets. There wasn't a lot of money in it, but my father and I enjoyed doing it. Years later, I jumped on the gold mining craze. There's a mine up in Alaska I worked in, but it's abandoned now. Made some good money doing that."

She gazed at me in awe. "That sounds like so much fun. I've always wanted to pan for gold. I can't imagine what it was like to live during that time."

"It had its perks, but I also endured great losses as well. Due to lack of medicine, the majority of my friends died young. It's something I had to get used to."

Tyla grabbed my hand and squeezed. "I know how you feel."

It was hard not to get attached to humans. Most of them were my good friends, especially when it came to my most profitable investment. "But a large chunk of my money comes from an investment I made many years ago. A friend of mine had owned an oil company but didn't have the money to buy the right equipment. I gave him the money and became his partner. When he passed on, I bought it outright and have owned the whole company ever since. It's one of the main suppliers of oil to both Canada and the United States."

"Wow." Her mouth gaped and she shook her head. "I don't think I can say any more than that."

"Good. Because it's show time. I think our guy just arrived." We both got up and the short, balding man who approached us held out his hand. He reeked of too much cologne and his beady gaze lingered on Tyla's chest.

She squeezed my hand. "No hurting him," she warned. "He probably doesn't see perky breasts at home."

"I don't give a shit if he's never touched a boob. If he stares at either one of my girls again, I'll rip his goddamn eyes out."

"You must be the Michaelson's. My name's Jeff Roberts. I believe you spoke with me on the phone," he announced. Tyla shook his hand and he beamed, but when it came to my turn, I made sure to squeeze it extra hard. He winced and pulled away. "Got a strong hold there, don't you, son?"

I clenched my jaw and showed my teeth in a forced smile. "We'd like to see the apartment you have available."

Pulling out a set of keys, he nodded toward the stairs. "Follow me, please." We got up to the apartment and he opened the door, walking in first. "The carpets have all been cleaned and the walls freshly painted. Our last tenant moved out about two weeks ago."

Here we go. "Why did they move? There's nothing wrong with the apartment is there?" I asked.

"No, not at all. He'd finally found a house and decided to move when the one year lease was up."

Tyla cleared her throat and he turned to her. "So everything's ready for us to move in?"

He nodded. "I can draw up the papers whenever you're ready."

"Sounds good," I said, grabbing Tyla's hand. "Just give us a day to think on it and we'll get back to you."

Jeff smiled. "As you wish. I look forward to speaking with you again."

I pulled Tyla in front of me so he couldn't watch her ass as we walked out the door. *Fucking cocksucker.* When we got to the car, Tyla reached for her phone. "You calling Blake?" I asked.

"Yep. I'm going to see if he can get a list of people who rented an apartment at this place over the past year."

It was a good move. Blake had access to all sorts of government programs, so finding the list of renters should be easy. Or at least I hoped. Time was running out.

SEVENTEEN

TYLA

"**A**re you sure you're okay?" Blake asked. "You've never asked me to do this kind of stuff before."

"I know. Just please trust me when I say I can't really explain it right now. Maybe one day I will."

He sighed. "I don't mind helping you, Tyla. When do you think you'll be coming back?"

"Hopefully soon. Call me when you find out something."

"Will do. Stay safe out there."

We hung up and I prayed he found something soon. Our options were running low.

"He's starting to ask a lot of questions," Sebastian said.

I slid my phone in my purse. "He's a cop, of course he's going to ask. The thing is, I know he'd keep our secret if I told him what we are."

"But you can't. Humans don't have the capability of understanding what we truly are. They see werewolves in the movies and in books, and would jump to conclusions. It's best we keep our secrets."

The reason I wanted to tell him was so I could stay at the ranch and work. I didn't want to have to move on somewhere else.

Taking my hand, Sebastian lifted it to his lips and kissed it. "I know you don't want to leave the ranch, but now that we're together, I can take you anywhere you want to go, give you anything you want. If you want your own ranch with your own horses, I can give you that. Just say the word."

"You'd do that for me?" I asked.

We'd just arrived back at the cabin. He shut the car off and faced me. "I'd do anything for you, love. All you have to do is ask."

"And I will," I said, getting out of the car. I looked up at the sky and could feel the moon drawing near. The power of it was stronger than it had ever been, pulling me toward Sebastian like a moth to a flame. At that very moment, the decision was made. I wanted to complete the bond, to be a royal.

Sebastian froze in his tracks and turned to me, his heated gaze fixed on mine. "You sure that's what you want?"

Wrapping my arms around his neck, I squeezed him tight. "With all my heart. Are you sure it's what *you* want?"

He chuckled. "You have no idea."

Once inside, he gave me my space so I could mentally prepare for the night to come. I sat by the window and attempted to read, but even my favorite pastime could do nothing to quell my nervousness.

The sky grew dark and the clouds gave way to the moon. It was the perfect night and almost time. Bonding with someone wasn't meant to be taken lightly. Thinking back to my time with Finn, I had been naive to even consider mating with him when I knew he wasn't my true mate. We would've been miserable.

Sebastian retreated outside while I went to the bedroom to take a shower. Before getting in the steamy, hot shower, my phone buzzed with an incoming text.

Bailey: Good luck tonight!

Me: What are you talking about?

Bailey: I just got off the phone with Sebastian. He sounds like a different man. Looks like there's a lot you need to tell me when you get back.

Me: What did he say?

Bailey: Only that I better not call back tonight. Have fun and don't do anything I wouldn't do. Love you! Be safe out there!

Chuckling, I sat my phone on the counter and hopped in the shower. Everyone back home had probably bet on the likelihood of me and Sebastian mating before we returned —*if* we returned. I had to believe we would.

The water felt amazing as it cascaded down my skin. I heard footsteps in the bedroom and half expected Sebastian to join me in the shower for a little foreplay before we sealed the deal. Unfortunately, that wasn't the case. The bathroom door opened slightly and I felt the cool breeze of the night air sift inside. I could smell the trees and the incoming snow that would arrive by morning.

"Sebastian?" There was no answer. What was he doing? I finished rinsing out my hair and turned off the water, grabbing the towel I had draped over the rack. The lights were off in the bedroom. "Sebastian?"

Wrapping the towel around my waist, I slowly tiptoed

to the door, heart racing. Why wasn't he answering me? I turned off the bathroom light and peeked through the slit in the door. Sebastian wasn't there, but the whole room was lit up with candles. The window was wide open, letting the moon shine its magic inside. It looked even more magical with the silky curtains blowing in the breeze.

Light footsteps sounded on the wooden stairs and I froze. When Sebastian walked through the door wearing only a pair of pants and carrying another candle, I breathed a sigh of relief.

"I'm not an intruder, you can come out," he said, setting the candle on the dresser. He stalked over to me and I trembled when he pulled me into his arms.

"You didn't answer me when I called your name. I was worried."

He brushed a hand down the side of my face, his blue gaze turning dark with need. "Anyone coming near this house would regret it if they tried. In fact, anyone who tries to stop us will meet a very slow and painful death."

"When you say it like that, it kind of turns me on." I chuckled.

His attention turned to the window and his eyes glowed. "It's time, love." Gripping the edge of my towel, he slowly pulled it away, letting it fall to the floor. A deep growl rumbled in his chest when his gaze raked over my body. "Are you ready for this?"

"More than ready." I stepped toward the bed and sat down, sliding across the silky sheets. Sebastian stood at the edge of the bed and unbuttoned his pants, letting them slide down to the floor. His thick length hung heavy between his legs and I had the overwhelming urge to taste him. My whole body trembled with need.

Keeping his gaze on mine, he crawled onto the bed and kissed his way up my body. Spreading my legs apart, he flicked his tongue over my clit, making me jerk. His warm breath blew across it as he spoke, making the yearning worse. "I feel like I've waited an eternity for this," he breathed.

I grabbed a handful of his hair and squeezed as he plunged his tongue deep inside. "Sebastian," I called out, close to losing control. But he stopped and smirked at me before licking a trail up to my breasts. "You are so evil. Luckily, two can play at this game."

I reached between his legs and wrapped my hand around his arousal, stroking his length. He sucked in a breath and pushed himself up and down inside my hand. The tip of his cock grew wet and I wiped the moisture away with my thumb. Licking my lips, I brought it to my mouth and closed my eyes, moaning as I tasted him.

Watching me suck on my fingers, he lowered his mouth to my breast and nibbled on its peak. "You'll be the death of me, love." He grazed my skin with his teeth, but didn't draw blood. I was glad he didn't. Whatever our next vision would be, I didn't want to see it on this night.

Reaching between my legs, he spread me wide and aligned himself at my opening. The moon glowed inside the bedroom, its magic swirling, like invisible threads all around us. I couldn't see them, but I could feel them. As soon as we completed the bond, those threads would be inside us, tethering us together. His magic would be mine, and mine his. I'd become a royal.

Pushing until he was as deep as he could go, I gasped and squeezed my legs tighter around his waist, pushing him farther in. We moved together as one, our bodies and minds fully connected. The bond we'd already opened up, floated to a whole new level. Our power merged and as each second passed, I felt stronger than I ever had before.

My insides tightened and I felt my release threatening to break free. Fisting his hands in my hair, Sebastian grunted with his hard thrusts, his cock pulsating inside me. I cried out as I finally reached the edge and trembled from the best orgasm of my life. Sebastian pounded his hips into mine as he chased his release, arms clutching me tight.

When he reached completion, I gasped as those magical threads bound us together. His soul was inside me and mine in his, unbreakable. I prayed if anything ever happened to him, death would take me as well. There was no way I could live without him from this day forward.

Leaning on his elbows, Sebastian bent down and kissed me, our bodies still connected. "I wouldn't be able to live without you either," he murmured against my lips. "I love you, Tyla."

Heart racing, I looked up at him and let the tears fall. "I love you too, Sebastian. I'm sorry it took so long for me to realize it."

He brushed the hair off my face. "Don't worry, love. We have the rest of our lives for you to make it up to me."

It was a task I was more than happy to accept.

EIGHTEEN

TYLA

The moment I woke up, everything was different. My vision was sharper, my mind clearer, and the bond connecting me and Sebastian together had never been stronger. I felt like I could lift a tractor trailer with no issues at all; although, I wasn't about to try it.

Sebastian rolled over and opened his eyes. "Good morning, love. How do you feel?"

"Amazing. You?"

He stretched and sat up. "Never better. And to think, you didn't want any of this."

I smacked him on the back. "Hey, I never said I didn't want it. I was just too scared to take it, only to lose it."

He turned and leaned over me, brushing the hair off my face. "There's something I haven't told you. I didn't want to bring it up because I was afraid you'd mate with me for the wrong reason."

"What is it?"

He glanced over at the blue stone sitting on the desk. The sun shone through the window, giving it a glow. "I talked to Seraphina the other day and she told me some-thing that might help us. Now that we've mated, it might actually work." He rolled to the side of the bed and fetched the stone. I wanted to touch it, but I didn't want it to suck me dry. Sitting back on the bed, he grabbed my hand. "Seraphina said that if we mated, our power would be stronger than the stone, that it probably wouldn't take your energy away as a royal."

Eyes wide, I gasped. "If it doesn't take away my energy, I can keep looking through it."

"Exactly," he mentioned happily. "Wanna try it and see what it does?"

Taking a deep breath, I closed my eyes and nodded. If I could look through the stone any time I wanted, there was more of a chance we could find Amelie. "Let's do it." When the stone touched my hand, I expected the jolt of electricity to suck away my power, but it didn't come. My mind opened up and I could see through Amelie's eyes. Sebastian squeezed my hand and I gasped. "I can feel you. It's not completely taking me under. Can you see into my mind?"

"Yes."

With my eyes still closed, I concentrated on the visions. Amelie was no longer in the dark basement, but in a car. There were bruises on her wrists but she wasn't restrained. She was in the front seat, looking out at the woods as they drove past. "That road looks familiar," I said.

I felt Sebastian jump off the bed. "That's because it's not far from here. She's on her way back."

Heart racing, I kept watching. "Who are you with, Amelie?" I whispered, hoping she'd turn her head. The next road they took was one I definitely recognized. "They're at her house!" How could that be? Something must've happened while Sebastian and I had been indisposed the night before. I was grateful for seeing the visions, but wished I could hear. It was like everything was on mute. "Maybe this is just a memory?"

"It can't be," Sebastian said as they pulled up to the house. "The dead wolves are still in the driveway."

I wanted to jump up and get dressed, but I had to see more. "Dammit, Amelie, who are you with?" She got out of the car and rushed over to the wolves, bending down to look at them. When she looked up, I got a good look at the man she was with. "It's Jaret. He must've saved her in the middle of the night. We have to get over there." Excitement bubbled in my chest. Amelie was back.

Opening my eyes, I dropped the stone on the bed. Sebastian was already dressed in a pair of jeans and a white T-shirt, and I couldn't help but smile. He was so unbelievably sexy. I'd never seen him in a pair of jeans, only slacks and nice shirts.

He held out his arms and grinned. "I do own jeans, love. I just choose not to wear them. Although, by the way your eyes just flashed, I will have to reconsider."

"Definitely. I'd tell you to fuck me right now, but we don't have time. I'm dying to see Amelie." Rushing out of bed, I threw on some clothes and followed Sebastian downstairs. By now, Amelie probably already knew I was in town. She'd be able to smell my scent around her house. "I need to call Finn," I said as we headed out the front door. "He's supposed to show up today with whoever's left from our old pack."

We were only a couple of miles away from her house,

and I felt like I couldn't get there fast enough. We got in the car and Sebastian went as fast as he could. My legs shook and I couldn't sit still as I dialed Finn's number. He picked up on the first ring.

"Hello?"

"Finn, I have some good news."

"What, you miss me?" Sebastian growled low in his chest, but thankfully, the rage was gone. I didn't have to worry about him ripping Finn's head off.

"Very funny," I said, shaking my head. "Where ya at?"

"A couple of hours away. Is everything okay?"

"I think so. Amelie's back in town with Jaret and we're headed that way. I have no clue what's going on. Can you meet us out there?" I asked.

"You got it. We'll be there soon."

We hung up and I blew out an impatient sigh. "I just want to know what happened," I said, glancing over at Sebastian. "Do you think she'll want to come back to Wyoming with us?"

He shrugged. "Depends on her mate, *if* they're actually mated that is. It's not just her decision." I just hoped she'd want to come with me. My aunt and uncle were gone. She needed to be with her family.

My phone rang. "Hey, Blake."

"You sound a lot happier this morning." He laughed.

Sebastian winked and grabbed my hand. "Maybe a little," I said. "Things are looking up out here. I should be coming back soon. What's up?"

"I looked up the information on apartment rentals at that establishment. Of course, I wasn't able to find a renter named Jaret Bleddyn, but there was another Jaret. Do you think maybe you got his last name wrong?"

I could still see his name in Amelie's journal. "It was definitely Bleddyn."

We started down Amelie's gravel driveway and her house slowly came into view. There was a black SUV there but no sign of Amelie or Jaret. Sebastian parked the car and we got out.

Blake sighed and I could hear him typing away on his computer. "Well, the other Jaret I found isn't from around the North Carolina area."

"Who is he?" I asked, walking toward the house.

"His name is Jaret Connery. It looks like he's a native of California, but moved to North Carolina this past year. Does he sound like the right guy?" The second I heard his name, I froze. How the hell could that be possible? The wheels in my mind turned, and with everything Finn had told me, it all started to come together.

"Tyla?" Blake called.

"I'm here. Sorry about that. Thank you for looking into this for me. I think I have everything I need."

"Anytime. Just call me if you need anything else."

As soon as we hung up, Sebastian grabbed my arm. "We have to get out of here," he demanded, voice low. That was when we saw them, glowing eyes staring back at us from the woods.

"I think it's too late."

The door to Amelie's house slammed open and she ran to me as I stepped out of the car, arms wide open. "Tyla, oh my God, I have so much to tell you!" She barreled into me and I breathed her in—she was mated. *Fuck.* I had to get her away from there as fast as possible. She breathed me in and gasped. "You're mated too? This is amazing."

I squeezed her against me, my voice a rushed whisper in her ear. "There's no time to explain. I need you to get in the car and come with us now." She tried to pull away, but I was prepared to drag her if need be.

"Tyla, what are you talking about? Let me go."

Dragging her it is then. "You're coming with me," I growled. We turned around and I froze. Sebastian stood in front of us, ready to fight as a guy we didn't recognize stared back at us with an evil leer on his face.

"You're not going anywhere," the guy said.

Sebastian's voice grew dark and hard. "Wanna bet?"

Amelie gasped. "What's going on? Who are you?"

More wolves filed out of the woods and surrounded us, most in wolf form, but some were still human. Those men flanked us. *"We can't fight them all and live,"* I said to Sebastian.

"No, but I don't think they plan on keeping us alive anyway. If Finn were here, we'd have a fighting chance." Finn was still a couple of hours away. We were screwed.

"Tyla, what's going on?" Amelie cried. She turned around and I heard her breathe a sigh of relief. Heavy footsteps fell on the gravel driveway behind us and I closed my eyes, knowing very well who it was going to be. "Jaret!"

She pulled away and I lost my grip. That was when I saw him. Amelie was in his arms, but he smirked at me over her shoulder. When his gaze turned to Sebastian, everything changed. The smirk faded and his eyes flashed.

"This must be my lucking fucking day," Jaret spat, voice full of venom.

Now that I saw him in person, there was no way I could deny who he was. He looked exactly like his father, Vincent Connery, the man who'd slaughtered my pack just to get to me. They had the same dark hair and evil hazel eyes.

I glanced up at Sebastian. *"Why is he looking at you like that?"* The Connery's were after *my* old pack, not him. Sebastian had nothing to do with Finn's people.

Sebastian closed his eyes for a second and I caught a glimpse of his memories. A girl appeared, her golden red hair shining in the sun as they played in a meadow. They were just kids, but his brothers were there as well. She wasn't a wolf, but something different. Then his visions shifted to a time many years later, in a clearing in the middle of the woods. It was a battle I had fought in.

"Why didn't you tell me?"

Sighing, he met my gaze. *"I didn't know."*

"Who was the girl?" She was beautiful and I could tell he cared about her.

"She was a friend. I'll tell you all about it later."

Amelie stepped back from her mate, grabbing our attention. "Jaret, who are all these wolves?"

He didn't even acknowledge her, choosing instead to step around her. The look of hurt on her face infuriated me. If he so much as hurt her, I was going to kill him. Amelie turned to me for answers, but I was in shock. Sebastian's memories had changed everything.

Jaret stalked forward, his glare split between the both of us. Sebastian's power surged through his body and shot out toward Jaret, making him stop before he could get too close. "I've been searching for you for years and here you are," he sneered. "Who would've thought you'd be mated to the one bitch who started it all. Now all I need to figure out is if I want you to watch her die or vice versa. Decisions, decisions."

Sebastian growled, making the wolves around us grow restless. They were poised to attack. "It's going to be real hard to make that decision when I'm ripping your head off."

Amelie sucked in a breath, her eyes wide. "Will somebody please tell me what the hell is going on?"

Down the way, I heard a car treading down the gravel driveway. It was too soon to be Finn. Dread settled in the pit of my stomach. A van with no windows in the back approached the house.

Jaret chuckled and waved his hand at the driver. "There will be plenty of time to explain, my darling. I'm sure your cousin will be more than happy to fill you in. Right now, it's time to go for a ride."

The wolves closed in around us while one of the guys opened up the back door to the van. Amelie started to go to him, but one of the wolves jumped in the way and snapped at her. "Jaret!"

"Get in the van, Amelie, or Adrian here will take a bite out of her." He pointed at me and I snarled. No one was going to touch me.

With tears in her eyes, she glanced back at me before getting in the van. I nodded to let her know everything would be okay. We were outnumbered; we had no choice but to play his game for the time being.

"You're next," Jaret said, glaring at me and Sebastian. The wolves moved in closer, baring their teeth. There were only ten of them, but it was still too many for me and Sebastian to handle on our own. I was stronger mated, but even having a royal's strength had its limits.

"If you so much as hurt Amelie, I'll rip out your balls and watch you choke on them before tearing you apart," I hissed. Jaret burst out laughing and Sebastian grabbed my arm.

"Don't provoke him," he warned. *"Get in the van and I'll follow you in. I'll handle that fucking cocksucker."* Huffing, I started toward the van with him close on my heels.

"Wait," Jaret called.

We turned and watched as he approached, several wolves in tow. My stomach clenched as I watched him leer at me, his gaze raking down my body. Sebastian's body trembled in rage, but I grabbed his hand, hoping it'd calm him down. It didn't work.

Jaret nodded at the other car and waved for me to follow him. "I change my mind. I want you with me. Let's go."

Sebastian's eyes flashed. "Fuck that. She doesn't go anywhere without me."

Jaret laughed. "Well, I say she does. It'd be a shame to rip her apart right now. The two of us have so much to catch up on."

"If you fight, they'll hurt you, Sebastian. Whatever Jaret throws out, I can handle it. I need you with Amelie. She needs to know what's going on."

He squeezed my hand and I looked up into his troubled gaze. "It kills me to know you'll be alone with that bastard. The thought of him touching you . . ."

"I'll be fine, I promise. You know I'm strong."

"The joys of bonding. Let me guess, you're talking about how much you love each other?" Jaret taunted.

"Like you would know anything about that," I snapped, glaring at him over my shoulder. I turned back around and several of Jaret's men stormed toward us. *"You need to go. Tell Amelie everything."* They were about to grab for him, but he jerked out of their hold.

"I wouldn't do that if I were you," he warned, backing up to the van. They stepped away and he got in, keeping his gaze on mine until they slammed the door. The van pulled away and my heart sank with the fear of never seeing him again.

NINETEEN

SEBASTIAN

"Fuck, fuck, fuck." The doors slammed and I couldn't see her anymore. *"Keep your mind open to me, Tyla."* I knew she could take care of herself, but I had to know she was okay. If I would've known for a fact she'd be safe, I'd have killed every one of those fucking wolves.

"I will. I'm getting into Jaret's car now. Don't worry about me, just please focus on Amelie."

Amelie sat in the corner of the van with her hands over her face. I felt sorry for the girl. Turning to her, I tried to get her attention. "Amelie?"

She lowered her hands. "I'm so confused. Why would Jaret do this? He said he wasn't part of a pack."

This was one of the very reasons every wolf needed to belong to a pack. She had no defenses being out here on her own. "He lied to you," I said. "His real name is Jaret Connery, not Bleddyn. I believe you know who his father is."

"Oh my God," she cried, slapping a hand over her

mouth just as Tyla did when she was upset. "I think I'm going to be sick."

She doubled over and I rushed to her side, putting my arm around her. "You didn't know," I soothed. She coughed and dry heaved, but nothing came up. Her despair was all I could feel.

"Why would he mate with me?"

Thoughts of my friend Alina plagued my mind. She too had been taken by a Connery, and paid the ultimate price. I wished every day I could turn back time and save her, but I'd failed. "To follow in his father's footsteps; it's what he grew up watching. But in your case, it was probably more about revenge. He's been killing your people for years, including your parents."

She cried even harder and shook her head. "They'd warned me something wasn't right. I should've known it was wrong when I couldn't hear his thoughts. The signs were all there. And now my parents are dead because of me."

"That's not true, Amelie. Connery was coming after you no matter what. You just happened to be the one he picked to charm."

"And I fell for it," she spat. Her overwhelming sadness had morphed into intense anger. "What's worse is, I believed the asshole. How could I be so stupid? I trusted him and his sister. Other than Tyla, she was my best friend."

My pulse spiked. "Sister? What does she look like?"

Amelie wiped her face off on her shirt. "Beautiful. She has silky red hair, and blue eyes. Not exactly the look of a gray wolf, but she was one. I've never seen her shift though . . ."

That was because she took after her mother and Jaret probably brainwashed her. "Did she ever talk about her mother?" I asked.

She shrugged. "Only that she'd died a long time ago. She was obviously skilled in magic. Laila's very powerful as well. She taught me a lot about stones and their magical properties."

Reaching into my pocket, I pulled out the moonstone. "What about this one? Do you know anything about it?"

Eyes wide, she grabbed it. "It's Laila's. Where did you get it?"

"In your room. We found it on top of your journal. It's how we knew you were back."

She squinted and shook her head. "How?"

I pointed to it. "When Tyla touches it, she's able to see inside your mind. While you slept, she saw your dreams. While you were awake, she saw through your eyes. You were kept in a dark basement the past few nights."

As if the memories haunted her, she shuddered. "I don't understand. Why would the stone be linked to my mind?" She handed it back to me and I put it in my pocket.

"I don't know. Maybe we'll find out." One way or another, I needed to find Laila and tell her the truth.

"What is he going to do to Tyla?" she asked, turning her tear streaked face to mine.

My blood boiled. "I don't know. But whatever happens, I'm not going to stop until he's dead. You will never be free until he's gone."

TWENTY

My goal was to not give into Jaret, to ignore him, but of course my patience ran thin. He opened the back door and waved me in. What I really wanted to do was smack the leer off his face, but I was outnumbered. I had a feeling his wolves didn't care whether I was a male or female; they'd make sure I was punished.

"Any day now," he said.

From the tension in the air, they were expecting me to run. I never ran from a fight. Holding my head high, I slid into the middle seat and he joined me. There were two men up front, and two guys in the very back. I tried to clear my mind so Sebastian wouldn't know how dire my situation was. The last thing I wanted was for him to do some insane rescue attempt.

Once we were on our way to wherever it was they were taking me, I turned my body toward the window, intentionally ignoring them.

"Tyla Rand . . . it's *such* a pleasure to finally meet you," Jaret said coolly.

I scoffed. "I bet."

"It is. I kind of wish I'd found you first. We could've had lots of fun together." He touched my shoulder and I growled, slapping his hand away. His eyes flashed and he smiled. "Yep, it should've been you. No wonder my father was determined to have you."

"Your father was a sick bastard. I guess the apple doesn't fall far from the tree."

He burst out laughing. "I guess not. Don't worry though, you'll get to see just what I'm capable of. What makes it even better is that you're mated to the one man I've been hunting for the past thirty years. Did you know he was the one who killed my father?"

I could still see Sebastian's visions in my mind. He'd killed Vincent, but I had no clue why. Why had he been in California when he was supposed to be in Canada? And there was still the mystery of the red-haired girl.

"I didn't know," I answered honestly. "Sebastian wasn't associated with my pack. His agenda was all his own."

His eyes flared. "We would've won if it wasn't for him. He's going to pay for his actions."

My blood boiled. "What about what *you* did? Your father's the one who led the attack on *my* people over his greed." I snorted in disgust. "If anyone deserves vengeance, it's us. You're the one who's going to pay."

"I don't think so, sweetheart." He moved closer, twirling one of my curls around his finger. Feeling him touch me made me sick. "You see," he whispered in my ear, "I always get what I want. Wherever you are, Finn will follow. My men smelled him in the woods. If you tell me where he is, I'll make your death as painless as possible."

Everything inside of me trembled in rage. "Fuck off," I spat.

His jaw clenched. "You might regret saying that come tonight. We'll see how long you last."

Heart pounding, I turned away from him and kept my gaze out the window. Fear crept its way up my spine and I hated myself for feeling it. I didn't want to be afraid, but something about his words terrified me.

"I'm going to get you out of this," Sebastian said. *"Both you and Amelie."*

"How is she?"

"Not good. I can't imagine what that fuckhead's done to her. If he's truly like his father, we're dealing with a sociopath."

"How do you know him?" I asked.

"I didn't. I knew one of his mates."

"The red-haired girl?"

More visions of her flashed through his mind. *"She was special, Tyla, and he killed her. I had to make sure he paid for what he did."* And he did pay. I watched as he relived that night, showing me how he'd ripped Vincent apart, limb by limb.

But what really surprised me was what happened after. The battle was over, the rest of Vincent's wolves had retreated, yet Sebastian stayed back to tend to my pack. Many of my people were dead, but there were several who were wounded, including Finn. He'd carried him to safety along with the others and sat with them through the night.

"When I knew they were healed, I left before they woke up. I didn't recognize Finn until just now," he said.

My eyes burned but I held back the tears. I didn't want dipshit beside me to think I was crying because of him. "He's alive because of you, Sebastian. We both are. If it wasn't for you, I wouldn't be here. Vincent would've won."

"And he's not going to now. Whatever happens, I will get you out safe."

"Not without you."

We were in Virginia, headed deep into the woods. The driveway had to be at least a mile long, surrounded by nothing but trees. We'd finally caught up to the van Sebastian and Amelie were in and I breathed a sigh of relief. There was a man who let them out, but then another who bound their hands together. Amelie hissed in pain and

Sebastian clenched his jaw. I opened the door, desperate to get to them.

Jaret grabbed my arm, his claws digging into my skin. "Not so fast, sweetheart. If you don't want to see them in pain, all you have to do is tell me where Finn is."

"I don't know," I shouted, feeling my own claws lengthen.

"Suit yourself." He pulled me out of the car and dragged me over to Sebastian and Amelie. One of his men wrapped a rope around my wrists and it burned, my skin raw underneath. *Wolfsbane.* The rope was soaked in it. "Take them to the basement," he commanded. "I'll deal with them later."

He stalked off and Amelie shouted after him, but he ignored her. The look of pain on her face made my heart break. Even though my skin was on fire, I leaned into Sebastian until one of the men pushed us apart.

"Walk," he shouted. There were four men guarding us as we made our way toward the massive cabin. They were all gray wolves, most likely the survivors from the battle thirty years ago.

I breathed in as deep as I could go, hoping to sense other people around, but there was nothing. We were in the middle of nowhere. Sebastian was behind me, and Amelie was out in front, her shoulders hunched.

Instead of going to the main door of the cabin, we were led to one on the bottom floor, underneath the patio. It was dark inside, with cement floor and walls—exactly like the room Amelie had been kept in earlier.

"This can't be happening," Amelie gasped, glancing

around the room. There was a small cot and a clock in the corner, the same one as before.

The man in front of her turned and smiled. "You're more than welcome to stay here again. Unless you'd rather be with them?" he asked, nodding toward us.

Amelie turned her head and nodded. "Keep me with them."

He burst out laughing. "Okay. Just so you know, their living accommodations are going to be a little . . . different."

I could only imagine what he meant by that. The lights were bright as we walked through another room, and when he opened the door, I coughed. The room reeked of wolfsbane. There were plants in every corner of the room. We wouldn't die from breathing in the fumes, but it would surely burn our lungs.

There was also the scent of blood. Splatters of it were on the floor and in the separate cages scattered around the room. They allowed enough room to stand and lie down on the floor, but that was it. All of them were empty except one. When the captive lifted his head, I gasped. It'd been thirty years since I'd seen him last, but he looked the same. He was one of Finn's closest friends.

His eyes went wide and he jumped to his feet. "Tyla? Amelie?"

"Josef," I whispered. The guy beside me pushed me into the cell next to him and locked the door while the others secured Sebastian and Amelie in theirs. Josef faced me from his cell and I latched onto the bars, hissing as my hands burned. The bars had been soaked in wolfsbane. "Okay! We get it already. Don't you think you went a little overboard with the wolfsbane?"

They completely ignored me and walked out of the room, locking the door behind them.

Sebastian growled and touched the bars. "More like, afraid we'll kill them."

I turned to Josef. "What's going on? How long have you been here?" His clothes were torn and dirty, and covered in blood. But it wasn't his blood all over the floor.

"Only a day. Jaret's men found me in Tennessee a couple of days after Finn left, asking me to come back to his pack. I was on my way to join him when I was ambushed and brought here. They're trying to find him, but it looks like they found you instead."

"More like *me*," Amelie corrected.

He turned in her direction and sighed. "Where are your parents?"

Her eyes flashed. "Dead. They killed them. I'd called Tyla and told her we needed help, but all it did was drag her down with me." She dropped her head, tears splashing on the concrete floor. "I'm so sorry, Tyla. I never meant to bring you into this."

"It's not your fault," I murmured. "You didn't know what was going on."

"Does Finn even know?" Josef asked, glancing at us all before settling his gaze on mine. "When I talked to him, he said you were dead."

"It was a lie my aunt and uncle had told him."

Amelie's brows furrowed when I looked at her. "You can't be serious. Why in the hell would they do that? How did they even know Finn was alive? I thought he was dead!"

"He found them about twenty years ago. At that point,

my mother told your parents to tell him I was dead. They knew if he found me, he'd want me to be his mate."

Her gaze shifted to Sebastian. "And if that would've happened . . . you wouldn't have met him." She sighed and reached for the bars, but stopped short. "Tyla, I promise I didn't know. I would never lie to you."

I nodded. "I know, it's okay. It all worked out in the end. Finn and I talked about it. He knows the truth now."

"So you've seen him?" Josef asked.

"A couple of days ago, but I honestly don't know where he's at right now. If he can't track Jaret's wolves, there's no way he'll find us here."

"He'll find us," Josef said, taking a seat on the floor. "One way or another, they'll draw him in. They have the perfect bait." He looked directly at me.

TWENTY-ONE

TYLA

"*Tyla, wake up.*" Sebastian's voice echoed in my mind.

I didn't want to wake up. I wanted to imagine I was back at home and not sleeping on a hard concrete floor in my enemy's basement. "*I don't want to.*"

"*There's movement upstairs. I have a feeling we'll be having company soon.*" I sat up and rubbed my eyes. Amelie and Josef were still asleep, and Sebastian sat in the cell across from me, his gaze tormented. "*I hate seeing you like this.*"

"*I'm fine, I promise. I'll feel even better when I can rip Jaret in half.*"

"*You'll be waiting in line for that one, love. There's a special place in Hell for him, right next to his father.*"

I glanced around the room. There were two windows near the ceiling, but they were too small to even attempt to sneak out of. It didn't matter anyway because the cages hindered us from escaping. Even if we could get out, it'd take time to pry away the bars. That time would cost us our hands. *"How are we going to get out of here?"*

He looked around the room and shook his head. *"I don't know. We just have to wait it out."*

As much as I wanted to think we'd get through this living hell alive, I had to question it. There were no visions of a happily ever after when we'd shared blood. It was obvious what was going to happen. Sebastian jerked his head my way, his gaze heated.

"You don't know that, Tyla. I told you I'll get you out safely and I won't let you down."

"But what is my life without you? You're my mate, Sebastian. I'm not going anywhere without you. We fight together, we die together. The sooner you realize that, the easier this will be." I was prepared to die fighting. Jaret wasn't going to get anything from me.

Sebastian clenched his fists, his mind going in a thousand different directions. In his craze, I caught one particular emotion he was trying to hide from me. Guilt.

"What are you hiding from me?" Before he could reply, footsteps sounded down the stairs. "Amelie? Josef? Wake up." They both sat up and we waited. It was like they'd deliberately kept us guessing just to toy with us.

The door to the room unlocked and Jaret strolled in, freshly showered. Amelie turned her head, not even acknowledging him. He went straight to her cell and bent down. "Good morning, dear," he said to her. "The bed was awfully cold without you this morning."

It's a shame you didn't freeze to death," she spat.

Chuckling, he glanced over my way. "A few hours with you and your snarkiness rubs off on her. I might have to keep you both around a little longer, and make things interesting." Another of his men walked through the door and stood guard, while Jaret paced back and forth. Sebastian and I met his stare, not afraid to back down.

"Let's see, who should I pick first? It can't be you," he said to me. "I need you for the grand finale, and for your mate to watch." Sebastian's power blasted through the room, bringing Josef, Amelie, and Jaret's wolves to their knees. Jaret froze, sweat beading on his forehead.

It was only for a split second, but I saw how hard he was fighting the urge to kneel. Sebastian was stronger than him.

Clearing his throat, Jaret stood between Amelie and Josef's cells, ignoring the fact Sebastian almost put him to his knees. He looked at Amelie and then at Josef, pursing his lips. "I can't choose my mate because I'm not done with her yet. I guess there's no other option."

Amelie jumped to her feet, eyes wild. "Jaret, no!"

"Stefan, if you would please," Jaret commanded. Stefan brushed off his jeans from where Sebastian dropped him to his knees, and glared at him before doing his alpha's bidding.

Josef stood and released a heavy sigh. "It was good seeing you again, Tyla. I fear this is goodbye."

"No," I shouted. "You hang on, you hear me?"

Stefan grabbed his arm and wrapped him in a wolfsbane soaked rope. I could hear the burning of his skin, but he looked at me and smiled. "It was an honor serving the Redwood Pack. Make sure you pass the message along to Finn."

Jaret pushed him toward the door and stopped in front of my cage. "Let the fun begin."

Hours had passed and no one had been down to our dungeon. My stomach growled but I knew there'd be no food. I fought better when I was hangry anyway.

Sebastian looked to me, lifting his brows. "What does that mean?"

Even if we were locked in a basement, the way he said it made me laugh. "It's when you're hungry and angry at the same time. For a woman, it's a lethal combination."

"Don't I know that," he teased.

Amelie looked at him like he'd lost his mind. "What are you talking about?"

He pointed at me. "She said she was hangry. I've never heard that before."

Amelie shook her head. "But she didn't say anything." Then it clicked into place. "Never mind, I get it. You're true mates." She wrapped her arms around her stomach, averting her gaze.

"You'll find your true mate one day," I promised. "We can't help who we fall in love with. Jaret tricked you."

"And I fell for it. That never would've happened to you. You would've seen through his lies."

"Maybe, maybe not. I'm not Wonder Woman, Amelie. Who knows what I would've done if the situation was turned. You're just as strong and smart as I am. When we get home, the first thing I'm going to do is teach you how to fight. Sebastian and his brother can help too."

She looked back and forth between us. "That's just it, I don't have a home anymore. I thought it was here, but I was wrong. My parents are gone because of me and I'm mated to a psychotic bastard. Unless one of us can miraculously kill Jaret, I'm screwed."

"How do you feel about that?" I wondered.

Sighing, she ran her hands down her face, her eyes misting with unshed tears. "I loved him, Tyla . . . shit, or at least I thought I did. If I'm given the chance, I'll kill him myself. I'll only be free once he's gone."

"When do you think his sister will show up?" Sebastian asked her.

Amelie started to speak, but I cut in. "What's going on? What are you two talking about?"

Amelie sighed. "Laila is Jaret's sister. We were good friends, until she betrayed me. I haven't seen her in almost two weeks."

"The moonstone is hers," Sebastian added. "She's the one who linked Amelie's mind to it."

"How do you know that?"

They looked at each other. "Because she has magic,"

Amelie said. "She's . . . different. I don't know why she did it though."

"How is she different?" I asked her.

Footsteps approached and the door swung wide open. Stefan walked in with two other men and they unlocked my cage, moving to Amelie's next. Stefan grabbed my arms and pulled them behind me, wrapping my wrists with wolfsbane ropes.

"What are you doing?"

"Jaret wants you to be part of the entertainment tonight. The show starts in an hour." He nudged me toward the door, and I looked back at Sebastian.

"What about him?"

Stefan chuckled and pushed me and Amelie out of the door. "He's coming too, but we're taking extra precautions with him. Can't have him killing anyone."

"Be safe, Sebastian."

"I will, love."

We walked through the other room and out the door. There was a large barn down the path, nestled further into the woods. Amelie and I looked at each other, dread settling into the pit of my stomach. Hoots and hollers rang out from the barn and I could only imagine why. Josef was in there; I could smell him.

The door to the barn opened and three wolves stumbled out with beers in their hands. They broke into laughter as they watched us approach. I could smell their lust, in fact, I choked on it. If Jaret's idea of a party was to watch us be gang raped, he had another thing coming. With evil leers on their faces, the men stepped aside so we could walk in.

Amelie immediately found Jaret and closed her eyes. "I

may not be able to hear his thoughts, but I sure as hell can feel them."

"What is he doing?" I asked.

She opened her eyes and they flashed with anger. "He's mocking me. No doubt about how gullible I am. Maybe it's a good thing he can't hear my thoughts. If he could, he'd hear how small I think his dick is. The men in our pack were much larger."

Jaret's eyes blazed and I knew everyone in the room had heard her. Stefan and the other guy backed away when he approached us. He walked right past me and grabbed Amelie by the neck. "If you dare say anything like that again, I'll rip out your goddamned throat. I don't care if you are carrying my child."

I gasped, completely at a loss for words. She was pregnant?

Her lips quivered but she didn't back down. "Go ahead and kill me," she challenged. "I'd rather be dead than have to look at you every day for the next nine months."

"Anything for you, my dear." He turned his lethal gaze to Stefan. "Take them inside."

Stefan grabbed me by the arm, his grip achingly tight as he dragged me the rest of the way into the barn. I looked over at Amelie, despair and shame evident on her face. "Why didn't you tell me?"

"I just found out two weeks ago when Laila told me. Apparently, she can sense the baby inside me. I was so excited when I found out. Now I don't know what the hell I'm going to do."

"We'll figure it out, I promise. You won't go through it alone." If we did get out of this alive, would she even want the baby? What would she tell the child about their father? Unfortunately, she'd have some hard roads ahead.

There was a wall blocking our view, and when we walked past it, I thought I was going to be sick. Josef was naked, his arms and legs tied to the wall as if he was a giant X. There were lashes all over his body and blood dripping down his skin.

"What the hell are you doing to him?" I shouted. Stefan shoved me into a chair and Amelie landed in the one beside me.

Jaret came up from behind and put his arm around us both. "He's facing his punishment, just like you will when the time comes. The boys will love it when you're up there, spread apart and ready for the taking."

The thought terrified me, but I'd make sure I was dead before that could ever happen. "Doesn't say much for your pack if you have to tie women up just to fuck them. Didn't realize they were all pussies."

Stefan growled but Jaret chuckled in my ear. "I'd watch what I say if I were you. My men might decide they don't want to wait any longer." The second he said it, Sebastian's power could be felt throughout the room.

"You might want to watch what you say as well," I warned.

Jaret turned around and groaned. "What the fuck happened?"

Amelie and I looked over our shoulders. Eyes wide, I watched as Sebastian walked in, surrounded by four wolves; all of them were beaten and bloody. They slammed him down in the chair beside me while Jaret demanded to know what happened. I wanted to touch him, but my hands were still tied behind my back.

I nudged him with my shoulder and stayed there. I had to feel him. *"What happened?"*

He coughed up blood and spit it out. "They provoked me and I made sure they paid for it."

"What did they say?"

His anger flared. *"I don't want to talk about it."* He didn't want to talk about it, but I could see what happened as clear as day in his mind; he couldn't stop me from seeing. They'd said they were going to pass me around until I begged for more. Fucking assholes.

"I'll kill them before they can do that, Sebastian. I'm stronger now. They don't know what we're capable of."

He glanced over his shoulder at the men he'd obliterated. "Now they do. I did all of that damage restrained with wolfsbane. There's no way in hell they could do that, and they know it."

"Which makes you more of a threat. Only, now we have bigger problems."

Brows furrowed, he met my gaze. "Other than Josef being strung up like a puppet, what else is there?"

"Amelie's pregnant." He froze and blew out a sigh. *"Exactly. I can't imagine what she must be going through. Only now, I'm worried about Josef. What are they going to do to him?"*

Sebastian looked up at him. "I don't know, love. I just know it's not going to be good."

"Everyone, may I have your attention please," Jaret shouted. "That also means you there, in the front." It was like I was a child being scolded in school.

Amelie nudged me in the side. "He's talking about you." Clenching my teeth, I glared up at him and he winked. I'd never wanted to kill someone as much as I wanted to kill him.

"Now that I have everyone's attention, we can get started," he said. "I think we need to show our guests what happens to those who defy us." Gut clenching, I watched as two of his men walked up to Josef and smacked him around, while another urinated all over him.

Jaret kept his gaze on mine, waiting for a shred of emotion. Amelie was clearly upset, but Jaret didn't care about her reaction; he waited for me and Sebastian.

"He's taunting us," Sebastian said.

"I know. It's killing me not to say something."

"There's nothing you can do. We have to show him this doesn't bother us." With the bond, I could feel his emotions. He was just as enraged as I was.

"How do you stay so calm when I know you don't feel that way?"

He sighed. "Takes lots of practice. The older you get, the easier it becomes, especially in war. But believe me, I want to rip these fuckers apart just as bad as you do."

The sting of the wolfsbane rope was reminder enough there was nothing I could do. Stefan was close behind us, laughing as more of the wolves strutted up to Josef to piss on him. Taking a deep breath, I averted my gaze, hoping it'd quell my anger—nothing helped.

"Eyes upfront," Jaret commanded. I looked up and he grinned in satisfaction. "I think it's time for round two." Rolling up his sleeves, he turned his focus to Josef. Josef lifted his gaze, jaw clenched tight. He was always a strong wolf, but not an alpha. This was a fight I knew he wouldn't win.

"Where's your alpha?" Jaret asked. Josef stayed silent and he paid the price. Jaret's claws extended and he swiped them across his chest. He hissed in pain, but stood strong. "I'm going to ask again, where's your alpha?"

Josef looked him in the eyes and spat in his face. "I'm not telling you a goddamn thing."

Jaret reared back and swiped his claws so hard across Josef's face, I heard bones in his neck crack. His cheeks were so badly torn, I could see teeth and bones. Amelie gasped and burst out crying. I wanted to cry too but I couldn't.

"Why don't they just go searching for Finn if they want to find him so fucking badly? Why do this?" I asked.

"They get off on torturing people. This isn't the first time they've done this."

"What do you mean?"

He glanced over at me and I could see the pain in his face. "After they took you from the basement, I heard some of the others talking. They've done this to several of the wolves in your old pack, including the women." My whole body shook with rage. *"They'll pay for what they've done, love. I promise."*

"I just hope Finn gets here so we can tear them apart."

"Speaking of Finn, there's something you need to know."

I jerked my head in his direction. *"What is it?"* A groan sounded from the front and I turned my gaze back to Josef. Jaret had clawed him again, only this time, it was across his back. I could smell the blood as it oozed down his body and pooled on the floor. *"Tell me."* I looked back to Sebastian.

"They can't find him."

"What do you mean they can't find him? Is it because he's so fast?" Finn was a master at fighting strategies.

He shook his head and my stomach dropped. "No, it's more like they can't trace him. His scent is nowhere to be found, not even at Amelie's. He's disappeared."

"But he wouldn't leave us like that. I know he can trace our scents."

He shrugged. "I'm not so sure about that. This group has the ability to hide scents. And if Finn's taken off, we're going to have to find a way out of here on our own."

There was no way Finn would just up and leave without knowing Amelie and I were okay. But we'd left no sign of struggle at her house, so maybe . . .

"Looks like it's time for round three," Jaret announced happily. He was covered in splatters of red, and instead of staying next to Josef, he waltzed over and took a seat beside Amelie. "Be sure to watch this, babe. This is what'll happen to you if you don't cooperate."

I scoffed in disgust, opening my mouth to speak but Sebastian beat me to it. "I'm sure it'll happen no matter what we do," he stated matter-of-factly. I seriously needed to learn how to control myself like that. *"I'll teach you,"* he promised.

"How are we supposed to cooperate if we don't know where Finn is? Looks like your men can't find him either. Maybe he tucked tail and ran," I spat.

Finn wasn't the type to back down, but he also didn't know it was the Connery's after us. I never got the chance to tell him. And maybe Sebastian was right. Their scents had been masked at Amelie's house. He could've easily thought we'd taken Amelie and left town.

Jaret huffed. "One way or another, I'll get him here. I have everything in place. We just need to see if he takes the bait."

"Then why torture Josef when you know how to get Finn here?" I growled.

"Because," he turned to me with an evil smile, "I enjoy it." Jumping to his feet, Jaret strolled over to where four of his men were taking off their clothes. He whispered something to them, but I couldn't hear what he said. Josef stood tall, even though I knew he was in tremendous much pain. His gaze met mine and I swallowed hard.

"I'm sorry," I said, mouthing the words.

He nodded once and took a deep breath. Jaret's men had already shifted and took their places around him—two in front and two behind. They snarled, baring their teeth, but Josef paid them no mind. This went on for about five minutes and when Jaret didn't get the reaction he wanted, he waved his hand in the air. The wolves attacked and I closed my eyes, the sound of flesh ripping and shouts of laughter were all I could hear.

Screaming, Amelie hid her face in my shoulder, her body shaking. When I opened my eyes, I really wished I hadn't. Josef was torn to pieces, his arms and legs still hanging from the ropes.

From across the room, Jaret nodded at Stefan and he grabbed me and Amelie by the arms, lifting us up. Sebastian growled and stood up with us. Jaret made his way over, grinning from ear to ear. "Did you like the show?" he asked.

"I will when it's you being ripped apart," I replied

angrily.

He burst out laughing and grabbed my neck, squeezing it so hard I couldn't breathe. Sebastian lunged, but he was held back by three of Jaret's men.

"Leave her alone!" Amelie cried.

Stefan pulled her away, and Jaret jerked me closer. "It's your turn tomorrow, bitch. I can't wait to play with you." Clutching his hand tighter, he held me in place, closing his lips over mine. Sebastian's anger flared as I tried to fight him, but there was nothing I could do. He bit my bottom lip and I cried out as he sucked down my blood, moaning and grinding himself against my hip. As soon as he let my neck go, I jerked my head away.

"You son of a bitch," I growled.

Chuckling, he licked his lips. "What I should do is kill these two," he said, pointing at Sebastian and Amelie, "and take you for myself. I could have so much fun with you."

I spat on the ground, hoping to get his taste out of my mouth. Sebastian tried to fight against the men but they dragged him away while Stefan took Amelie. Now I was alone with him. "Surely you're not afraid to take me on yourself, are you?"

"And that's what I like about you. You're a fighter, not like Amelie, who cowers in fear."

My temper flared. "She loved you and she's pregnant with your child. You'd kill them just to have me?"

"You're a lot stronger than she is, an alpha. The son I give you will have both of our strengths. If everything goes according to plan tomorrow, I might just have to think about this." Grabbing my arm, he pulled me out of the barn and back to the cabin. I had no clue what the hell to do.

TWENTY-TWO

TYLA

I nstead of going in through the basement door, Jaret took me up to the main level. "Where are we going?"

"You're staying with me tonight."

"Fuck no, I'm not," I hissed.

He dragged me in through the door, where Stefan waited on us. "Disobey me and my men will go straight downstairs. Who will you choose to live? Your pregnant cousin or your mate?"

Deep down, I knew who I'd choose, but I didn't want to say it. "Fine."

"Tyla, where are you?" Sebastian asked. I could feel his desperation through the bond.

"I'm upstairs with Jaret."

"What the hell are you doing up there?"

Swallowing hard, I followed Jaret down the hall to a bedroom that smelled exactly like him. I tried to get the thoughts out of my head, but Sebastian kept pushing to get in. I didn't want him seeing what was about to happen.

"Tyla! Stop pushing me out."

Stefan stood guard at the door while Jaret shut it, locking us in. When he turned to me, he raked his hungry gaze down my body. "Turn around," he ordered.

"Why?"

He pulled a pair of gloves out of his back pocket and slipped them on. "Not unless you want to stay in that rope for the rest of the night. Personally, I don't want my sheets covered in wolfsbane."

"Well, in that case, I'll keep it on."

Huffing, he stalked toward me but I had nowhere to go. *"Tyla, answer me!"* The sound of Sebastian screaming echoed in my head. Grabbing my arm, Jaret turned me around and pushed me onto the bed, pinning my body beneath his. I was stuck with my face buried into the mattress. All I could smell was his scent, it surrounded me like a dark cloud. The ropes pulled against my skin and I hissed in pain as he roughly untied me. When the ropes fell to the floor, he jerked me back to my feet.

"Does that feel better?" he asked, slipping off the gloves.

I looked down at my wrists, they were blistered and red. "Not exactly."

He bit his lip and smirked. "Then maybe a shower will help. Take off your clothes."

"You've lost your fucking mind," I hissed, taking a step away.

"Tyla!"

Eyes burning, I took a deep breath. *"I'm sorry, Sebastian."* With newfound strength, I shut him out. It broke my heart to do it, but I couldn't let him in my head, not when there was nothing he could do to help me.

"Shall I get Stefan to bring your mate up to watch?"

When I didn't answer, he started toward the door. "Stefan," he called.

"Stop," I pleaded. "I'll do it. Just don't bring Sebastian in here."

Grinning, he turned back around. "I knew you'd see it my way."

I took off my clothes and faced him head on, ready to shift at a moment's notice. If he tried to get anywhere near me with that dick of his, I wasn't going to let him win, not without a fight.

A satisfied moan escaped his lips as he looked at me. "Very nice. Now get in the shower and clean up for me. You smell like your mate." The bathroom was off to my right and before he could follow me in there, a knock sounded on the door. "What is it?" Jaret growled.

"Your sister's back. She wants to see you," Stefan answered.

"Where the hell has she been?"

"Don't know. She says it's urgent though."

Huffing, he turned back to me and pointed at the shower. "Clean up. I'll be right back."

As soon as he left, I switched on the shower and searched through the drawers, looking for anything I could find to help defend myself. When I found nothing, I rushed into the shower. My wrists burned where the ropes had rubbed me raw, but thankfully, the water washed away the painful wolfsbane residue.

Stepping out of the shower, I froze. There was someone in the bedroom, but it wasn't Jaret. "Who are you?" I inquired. I couldn't see who it was, but I could hear them.

I walked out of the bathroom and there was a girl with

her back to me. She had red hair hanging down in waves past her shoulders, dressed in a long, white skirt and white top. She was a wolf, but she was something else as well. "Laila?"

She set the tray down and turned around, holding a steaming mug in her hand. Her face looked familiar, like I'd seen it before. "Amelie must've told you about me."

I snorted. "More like how you betrayed her. What do you want?"

Sighing, she stepped toward me. "I'm here to help you. There's a change of clothes on the bed. Now get dressed, and hurry." I did as she said and threw on the clothes. The last thing I wanted was to be naked in Jaret's bedroom. "And I didn't betray Amelie. She's my friend."

"That's not what she thinks. Your family's full of fucked up psychopaths. She's not going to believe you for a second."

Laila closed the distance between us. "I don't have time to explain. Drink this." She held the mug out to me. It wasn't coffee and it wasn't tea.

"I'm not drinking that shit."

"Dammit, Tyla, I'm trying to help you. I need you alive and the only way to do that is to keep you from fighting Jaret. This is the only way. Now drink."

Keeping my gaze on hers, I took my chances and drank the contents. It tasted like hot peach green tea. Once I was done, she took the cup and set it on the dresser. "What happens now?" The room started to spin and she took my hand, guiding me over to the bed. My head hit the mattress and everything began to fade.

Her voice sounded far off, but I could still hear her.

"You're going to sleep for a while. Just know that you're safe. No one's going to touch you." She held my hand and then a zing of pain sliced through it. I could smell my blood. "I've been waiting my whole life for you to show up and now you're here. Soon it'll all be over."

TWENTY-THREE

SEBASTIAN

"Sebastian, please wake up."

My head pounded and all I could smell was burnt flesh. I opened my eyes and saw Amelie, her tear streaked face wild and desperate.

"Oh my God, I thought you were dead," she cried.

Groaning, I sat up and hissed when I looked at my hands. The skin was peeled back and they reeked of wolfsbane. "What happened?" It was all a blur, until I looked at the bars and everything came crashing down. "Tyla!" Closing my eyes, I concentrated on her, but it was like she wasn't even there. "No!" I shouted.

"Where is she?" Amelie demanded, getting to her feet.

I looked up at her. "I don't know. I can't feel her in my mind. All I remember is trying to get out and then everything going blank. What happened?"

She shook her head. "I'm not sure. You were doing that mind to mind stuff with Tyla, then you went crazy. The next thing I knew, you'd wrapped your hands around the bars and started prying them apart. I screamed for you to stop, but you didn't listen. Your hands kept burning. Then suddenly, you stopped and fell to the floor."

"How long was I out?"

"I'm not sure exactly, but it felt like forever."

My stomach clenched. Tyla had been alone with Jaret for who knew how long. If anything happened to her, I'd never forgive myself. Kneeling down on the floor, I covered my face with my mangled hands. "Fuck, fuck, fuck. Why isn't she answering me?"

As if on cue, Jaret and three of his men walked in. When he got sight of the cage and my damaged hands, he barked out a laugh. "Not too happy this morning, I take it?"

"Where's Tyla?" I growled. The wolfsbane had definitely taken its toll on my body. I felt the poison eating its way through my hands. Stefan opened the cage door while the other two pulled me out and slammed me into a chair. Before I could go on the attack, they wrapped a large rope around me, tying me to the hard, wooden chair. As bad as I wanted to shift, I couldn't. There was too much wolfsbane on my body, weakening me.

Leaning against the wall, Jaret smiled. "Tyla's still sleeping soundly in my bed." Then his gaze met Amelie's. "I made a mistake in choosing you. Your cousin knew exactly what to do to please me." He licked his lips. "I can still taste her."

My whole body shook with rage, my insides on fire. "You son of a bitch," I growled. "If you've touched her in any way, I'll rip off your goddamned head."

"Oh, I did more than touch her," he claimed, grabbing

his crotch. "Many times actually. Can't you smell her on me?"

Amelie's screamed, "No! How could you do that?" I could smell her scent on him and it only fueled the fire more.

Jaret walked over to her and grinned. "Simple. I spread her wide and fucked her. She was begging for more by the time I got done."

Even though it burnt her skin, Amelie reached through the bars and smacked him. "I hope you rot in Hell."

He rubbed his cheek and winked at her before coming back to me. "Once tonight's over, I'll kill you both and not have to worry about you getting in the way. Then, when I've gotten what I want from Tyla, you can reunite in the after-life. But first," he nodded at his men, "it's time for a little fun. Some would call it payback."

Amelie gasped, her eyes wide. "Jaret, stop! Don't do this."

His men surrounded me, two of them holding me to the chair. Jaret reared back and punched me in the jaw, the sting of it burning like fire. My head snapped to the side, but it wasn't enough to deter me. Jaret cracked his neck and approached me, his eyes and claws shifting.

"That was for me." He cracked his knuckles. "This is for my father." He punched me again, then slashed his claws across my chest. Blood oozed through my shirt as my skin split open. Before he could hit me again, his attention was drawn to the door opening. "What the hell are you doing in here?" he growled.

"Just checking on you, dear brother." The voice

sounded like music. I couldn't see her, but judging by the look on Amelie's face it had to be Laila. "I thought you could use some help. You need to conserve your energy for tonight. Besides, you have a lot to get prepared."

Clenching his teeth, Jaret huffed and backed away. "Be sure to make it exponentially painful."

She laughed and it sounded exactly like her mother's. It pained me to think of Alina's child as being evil. "Don't worry about me. I know what to do."

Jaret walked out of the room and so did the other wolves, their footsteps hard and determined as they left the house. I couldn't hear anyone else moving around, not even Tyla.

"You are such a conniving bitch," Amelie hissed. "I trusted you."

"I'm not your enemy," Laila replied softly.

Amelie scoffed. "Liar. You better hope I don't get out of here. You'll be one of the first ones I kill."

I heard Laila's steps edging closer. I saw the wolfsbane plant in her hand before I looked up at her face. She looked exactly like her mother, the same red hair and slender body . . . but her eyes were different; they were blue instead of green. I felt like I'd been kicked in the gut. I recognized them. They weren't Vincent's, but another's. I wondered if she knew the truth.

"Plan on using that on me?" I asked, hooking a glance at the plant. How was she even able to hold it?

She tossed it to the floor. "Looks like you've had enough already."

"Like you care," Amelie grumbled.

Laila rolled her eyes and freed me from the rope. "I wouldn't be down here risking my life if I didn't."

"Where's Tyla?" I demanded. "What's happened to her?"

She pulled out a vial. It smelled like Tyla's blood. "Hold out your hands." I did as she said and she dropped a few drops of the blood on each open wound. My burns healed up as if nothing had ever happened. "Tyla's fine. She's upstairs sleeping."

I jumped up, the chair slamming down on the floor. "What did he do to her?"

Laila backed away, holding her hands up in the air. "He didn't violate her, I promise. I wouldn't have let that happen."

"Then why does he smell like her?"

She sighed. "He got in bed with her this morning so her scent would be on him. It was just to get a rise out of you. When I got back into town last night and found out he'd switched plans, I had to do something. My only option was to give her a tonic to put both of you to sleep."

"How did it work on me?"

"I have a way of linking things. I knew you'd go crazy if you could see what was happening in her mind. That's why I made sure you passed out along with her. Jaret doesn't like sleeping with women if they aren't coherent. He likes the fight. If she'd fought him, he would've killed her, and then you would've died seeking retribution."

"Fucking cocksucker," I growled low.

She pointed to Amelie. "I was also the one who linked the moonstone to Amelie's mind. I knew you and Tyla would find it. It was the only thing I could think of to keep you informed and also keep my distance."

I pulled the moonstone out of my pocket. "What's the purpose of all of this? Are you with your brother, or against him?"

"You should know the answer to that, Sebastian. My mother loved you and your brothers."

We loved her too, but my affections weren't that of a lover. She had captured Zayne's heart when we were kids. I didn't tell my brother what'd happened to her until *after* I'd killed Vincent. Ever since then, he hadn't fully forgiven me for not telling him sooner. I also never told him she'd given birth to a child—a child I didn't believe to be his, until now.

"She died when you were an infant. How do you know that?"

She cringed at my words, her pain filling the room. "I'll tell you everything when time allows. Right now, you have to trust me."

"Don't believe anything she says," Amelie snapped. "She's no better than her brother. Can't you see it's just a scheme? Jaret probably put her up to it."

Tears filled Laila's eyes and she turned to Amelie. "I know you don't believe anything I'm saying, and I don't blame you. Just know, I've lost more than you could ever imagine. But your forgiveness is what I'll seek when all of this is over."

She paused and her gaze flitted down to her clasped hands before addressing her again. "And there is something you should know." She glanced at me and then back to Amelie, ashamed. "You're not pregnant."

Amelie gasped and clutched her stomach. "What are you saying?"

Releasing a shaky breath, Laila closed her eyes. "I originally told you and Jaret that because I knew it would keep you alive. It was the only thing I could think of at the time. The tea I gave you to drink each week had an herb in it to keep you from conceiving. I couldn't let him have that kind of hold over you."

Amelie dropped to her knees, tears streaming down her cheeks. "I'll be free of him then?"

Laila nodded. "As long as my plan works."

"Which is?" I asked.

"Getting us all out of here alive. I'll do everything I can to keep Tyla and the baby safe. But when the time comes, I'll need your—"

"Stop," I shouted, my heart racing. I looked over at Amelie and judging by her wide eyes she had to have heard what I did. "What baby?"

Brows furrowed, Laila glanced back and forth at us and then sighed. "I didn't realize you didn't know. But then again, I guess it is a little soon for that."

"Tyla's *pregnant*?" I asked, hardly believing the words coming out of my mouth.

Laila smiled and nodded. "It's not every day the father finds out before the mother."

Footsteps sounded from above and she gasped. "Dammit, they're back. I don't have time to explain the rest. Whatever I do, you need to play along, both of you." She tossed a quick glance at Amelie, before focusing on me. "This is probably going to be worse for you. Can you handle it?"

"You don't even have to ask." I would give up my life in an instant to save Tyla and my unborn child. They needed me and I wasn't going to let them down.

Laila nodded, her gaze sad. "Here we go." She closed her eyes and whispered words under her breath. The last thing I heard before the darkness took over was Amelie's scream.

TWENTY-FOUR

TYLA

I woke up in a daze, hoping everything that had happened was just a bad dream. Unfortunately, that wasn't the case. I found myself in Jaret's bed, reeking of his scent. I was fully clothed, and thankfully, untouched. If he had raped me in my sleep, there would've been nothing I could've done. Whatever Laila had given me to drink wiped me out. I looked at the clock, eyes widening at the time. I'd been out for almost twenty-four hours.

"Sebastian?" There was no answer, just a black void in my mind where he used to be. Panic set in. *"Sebastian!"* Where was he? Jumping out of bed, I started for the door, but it opened and Jaret waltzed in.

"Good morning, sunshine. Ready for the finale tonight?"

"Where's Sebastian and Amelie?" I demanded, refusing to answer him.

His grin widened. "Amelie's being taken to the barn as we speak. She's fine for the moment, but I can't say for how long. Sebastian, on the other hand, isn't doing so well. You should've seen his face when he smelled you on me and I told him I fucked you last night."

My body shook, fire bubbling in my veins. I needed Sebastian to hear me so I could tell him the truth. Why was our connection still gone? As hard as I could, I lunged and punched Jaret in the face. His head snapped to the side and he laughed. Before I could make another move, he grabbed me around the neck, his movements a blur. He was stronger than me.

"You think you can fight me?" he growled, pushing me back toward the bed. I couldn't breathe; his grip was too tight. Digging my claws in his hand, I was able to pry them apart to get some air.

"I know I can."

"Let's just see about that. How about we give your mate something to *really* be mad about?" He grabbed my shirt and yanked it up. The door burst open.

"Really?" Laila snapped. "Everyone's waiting for you. There'll be plenty of time to do whatever it is you want to do later. For now, you have to get ready."

Huffing, Jaret released my neck. "Fine. Let's go." He jerked me to my feet and dragged me out of the door. Laila didn't acknowledge me, keeping her face a stony mask. If she was trying to help, she wasn't showing it.

"Sebastian! Talk to me." Again I was met with silence.

Laila followed us outside, where two of Jaret's men awaited us. "Amelie's tied up and ready to go," one of them said.

"What?" I gasped. Visions of Josef tied up in the barn flashed through my mind. They'd ripped him apart. I couldn't let them do that to Amelie.

Jaret's eyes twinkled. "Don't worry, sweetheart. You're about to join her."

All I wanted to do was fight, but I couldn't do it on my own. We edged closer to the barn and I was so afraid of what I'd see when I got in there. Sebastian had to be okay. I couldn't afford to think otherwise. My cousin, however, was a different story. Jaret's men snickered behind me and it pissed me off. When we turned the corner, I froze mid-step. Amelie stood on the opposite side of the room, naked with her arms and hands bound in ropes, just like Josef had been.

"Amelie!" I shouted.

Her head snapped up. "Tyla."

"What kind of a sadistic fuck are you?" I growled at Jaret. "She's your *mate*."

He shrugged. "Not after tonight. By the next full moon, you will be. First though, I need your help."

"I'm not helping you do shit."

He chuckled and waved at his men. "I beg to differ. If you don't, you'll condemn your poor cousin to a fate worse than death." Leaning close, he wrapped his arms around my waist, his voice just a whisper. "My sweet Amelie . . . just look at her up there. She's so naïve and vulnerable, not the alpha you are. If you don't do as I say, I'll have every wolf in this room take a bite out of her as they fuck her until she breaks. Do you want that?"

My stomach clenched. I knew he'd do it. "No," I whispered.

"Then shut your fucking mouth."

His men grabbed my wrists and hauled me up to the front, where a set of ropes hung from the ceiling. They tied me up and left me dangling beside Amelie. Jaret's pack congregated in the barn, like it was just a normal party, drinking beer and gawking at us with their heated gazes. Some of the guys came up close. As one reached out to touch me, Jaret barked out an order.

"No one will touch the alpha but me. The other one is for you."

Amelie let out a whimper when the shortest guy of the group stepped up and sniffed her.

"You're lookin' real nice, all strung up and waiting for me." His buddies chuckled and swayed, leaning on each other as they continued to drink. "I'll bet you're already wet just thinking about my cock." He shoved his hand between her legs and she spit on his face. "You fucking bitch." He reared back and slapped her across the face. "Save it for later, you're gonna need something for that dry ass cunt, or it's really gonna hurt." The disgusting man and his groupies roamed over to the rest of their pack to take a round of shots.

I turned to Amelie. "Are you okay?"

She nodded. "I'll be fine. You?"

"No. I can't hear Sebastian. Where is he?"

Amelie's face fell and she turned her head, her gaze meeting something across the room. She sucked in a breath. It was Sebastian, I could smell him. I quickly turned to find him and wished I hadn't. He was slung over Stefan's shoulder. Walking up to us, he threw him on the floor in front of me, and I screamed.

"Sebastian!"

The others laughed as I stood there, screaming for him to wake up. He wasn't dead, but by the looks of him he could very well be soon. No wonder why I couldn't hear him. His face was burnt, like he'd been soaked in liquid wolfsbane.

I turned to Amelie, my voice unrecognizable to my own ears. "What did they do to him?"

"It wasn't them, it was her," she said, nodding toward Laila. "I heard some of the others talking. They knew that if Sebastian could see you up here, it'd ruin everything. Jaret doesn't want him dead yet." I could only imagine what his plans were for Sebastian.

Jaret turned our way and he grinned, his strides slow and confident. "You're right, I don't want him dead," he said as he walked up to her. "I want him alive long enough to watch me fuck his mate on the next full moon. That way, when we kill him, it'll be the exact moment she becomes mine. There's no sweeter revenge."

The thought made me sick.

"What happens to me?" Amelie asked.

Stefan walked up behind him and whispered something in his ear. His eyes went wide and he smiled. "Excellent. I guess it's time to get the party started." Ignoring Amelie, he turned around and lifted his hands in the air, grabbing everyone's attention. "Looks like we're about to have some company. Want to make his welcome worthwhile?"

The energy in the room spiked. Were they talking about Finn? Was he coming for us? I glanced down at Sebastian, my whole body warring with itself. On one hand, I was devastated and scared, but on the other, I was pissed and ready to go out with a bang. I didn't want to lose him.

"Sebastian, please wake up. I need your strength."

Jaret circled us and then stood behind me, burying his nose in my neck. He snaked his arms around my waist and chuckled in my ear. "How does it feel to know you're the one who brought him to his death?"

"Sebastian's a lot stronger than you think."

"I'm not talking about him."

Right then, I knew. Finn was walking into a trap and he probably already knew. It was a suicide mission. "What did you do?"

"It was simple really. We took your clothes and left them with a note at Amelie's house. We told him if he didn't come alone, we'd rip you apart. My guys said he's almost here." He was telling the truth. I could smell Finn slowly approaching, with no one by his side. It was going to be him against eight wolves.

Jaret moaned in my ear and cupped my breast, squeezing it through my shirt. "Looks like he needs a little encouragement." He snapped his fingers at his men and two of them stalked over to Amelie.

"Don't you fucking touch her," I shouted.

Jaret jerked my head to the side and growled. "They're going to do more than that, sweetheart. But it's nowhere close to what I'm going to do to you." He grabbed the back of my shirt and ripped it off.

I screamed as his teeth bit into my neck, his fangs tearing through my skin. The pain was excruciating, the blood flowing like crimson rivers down my chest. All throughout the room, eyes glowed and the energy spiked. However, there was one person I could feel more than the rest. *Finn.* He was there.

"Let them go," he yelled, appearing at the door.

Jaret ripped his teeth out of my flesh and laughed. "It's about time you showed up."

Finn met my gaze, his jaw clenched tight. He knew he was going to fight to the death. Tears slid down my cheeks as I glanced from him to Sebastian, lying motionless on the floor. They weren't going to let us go, it was never in the cards.

Finn held out his arms, marching right into the middle of the barn. "I'm here and I'm alone. It's what you wanted, right? Now take your revenge and let them go."

Jaret's men surrounded him. "The bitches are mine, Olcan. They're not going anywhere." He took off his shirt and tossed it on the ground, meeting Finn in the center. "You and I, however, are going to finish this once and for all."

Finn's eyes flashed. "Have it your way." Turning on his heel, he pushed through the others to march outside, ripping off his shirt.

Once they'd left the barn, the sound of howls filled the night air. I looked over at Amelie, who had blood dripping down both sides of her neck. She hissed in pain, but I could see the strength in her eyes. She was ready.

"We have to get out of here and help them," I said. "I can't let Finn fight my battle, not again. If I can just get down to Sebastian, he'll be okay." Amelie nodded, but then her gaze landed on something to the other side of me. A small smile spread across her cheeks and I froze.

"Not unless I get to you first," Sebastian murmured in my ear. Gasping, I turned my head, but he placed a finger on my lips. "Don't say anything. We don't want anyone to hear us." His eyes flashed and he growled when he saw my neck. He freed me from the ropes and pulled me into his arms.

"I don't understand," I cried, running my hands all over his face and chest. I missed the way it felt to be in his arms. But something had happened. His face was free of burns, and his energy was stronger than before. I could feel him in my mind; the link was open.

"Let's end this," a voice whispered from behind.

I turned around, ready to fight, only to find Laila cutting Amelie out of the ropes. Amelie even smiled at her. What the hell was going on?

Sebastian turned my face to his. "She's helping us, love. You can trust her."

"What happened? Just a few minutes ago it looked like you were close to death."

"It was a façade, a glamour of sorts. Laila put a spell on me to make me look like that. I was awake the whole time." His jaw clenched. "Even when that fucker bit you. Hearing your screams about killed me."

"There was no choice," Laila interrupted, pocketing the knife in her pants.

Sebastian tore off his shirt and dropped his pants. I started to do the same, but he grabbed my wrist. "Not this time."

"Have you lost your mind? You need me out there," I hissed low.

"No, he doesn't," Laila said. "The others are here."

I jerked my attention to her. "Who? There's no one else here, except Finn, who's going to get ripped apart if we don't get out there and help him."

She huffed impatiently. "Finn's pack is here. I found him earlier and explained everything. I then used the same spell I put on Jaret's wolves on his. That way, they could come in undetected. They're here, ready to fight."

Growls erupted outside and I heard a yelp. It was Finn. "Come on," I cried, jerking out of Sebastian's grasp.

He grabbed my wrists again, his glowing gaze full of heat. "You can't, Tyla."

"Why? I fight all the time."

His gaze shifted to my stomach. "Not while you're carrying my child, you don't. I can't lose you both. I'm not willing to take that risk."

"This is insane. You're not making any sense. Don't you think I'd know before you?"

"I felt your baby's energy last night when I gave you that tonic," Laila confessed. "I thought Sebastian should know what was at stake."

The more I looked at her, the more everything fell into place. I knew where I recognized her from. "I saw you in Sebastian's mind. It was a vision many years ago, but you were there."

She froze and quickly glanced at Sebastian before turning back to me. "It was my mother, not me. We're running out of time, let's go."

Now it was my turn to freeze. She had the same eyes as Sebastian. And as selfish as it may seem, I didn't want to think of him fathering another child other than our own.

Sebastian clutched my face in his hands. "You need to get out of here. *Go*," he commanded. "Keep our little one safe."

"I'll help protect her," Amelie promised.

I shook my head. "You can't."

She smiled. "I'm not pregnant, Tyla. Laila only told Jaret that to keep me safe. Now let me do this for you."

Sebastian kissed me and placed his forehead to mine. "I love you."

"I love you too."

He raced off and shifted mid-air, lunging at a wolf right outside the barn. Amelie shifted and nudged me with her nose. I turned to see Laila rushing to the back door of the barn. She held her hand up to stop us when we approached.

Listening intently, I couldn't hear anything other than the wolves out front, battling it out. "Where are we going?" I whispered. My wolf itched to break out and fight, and if I had to, I would in a heartbeat.

"My car. It's in the driveway. If I can get us away from here, we'll be safe."

"Why can't you just shift?"

She lowered her gaze and huffed. "I don't have that ability. I'm only half wolf."

"What else are you?"

Her blue eyes turned my way. "Fae. I guess I take more after my mother." Amelie whined, rubbing her head against her legs and Laila smiled down at her. "Thanks, Am. I've wanted to tell you for so long." Opening the door slightly, she looked around. "I think we're good. Let's go."

We followed her out and bolted toward Jaret's house. The driveway was around the front and we were almost there. Then a snap in the woods caught my attention. I turned to the noise just in time to see glowing hazel eyes lunging straight for Amelie.

TWENTY-FIVE

TYLA

"**A**melie!" I shouted.

She yelped as Jaret took her down to the ground. Then all was still.

I started to run to her, but Laila jerked me back and jumped over me, her knife poised in the air. She took off at a sprint, heading straight for Jaret, but he turned to face her at the last minute and smacked her with his claws. Flying through the air, Laila landed hard against a tree, the breath leaving her lungs. She gasped and tried to stand, but then fell back to the ground.

Jaret faced off with me, while Stefan shifted and jerked Laila to her feet. He grabbed her knife and held it to her throat, the blade biting into her skin. Jaret shifted and glared at her. "What the fuck are you doing?"

"Saving my friends," she spat. "They're my *real* family."

He scoffed. "How dare you turn your back on me. I'm the one who raised you."

"No, you used me. And it's time you paid the price. I'm

not going to let you and your father get away with what you've done. If he was still alive, I would kill him myself."

His anger blasted through us. "Traitor! He was *your* father too."

Tears fell down her face and she shook her head, the knife slicing her throat. Blood ran down her neck and she cried. "He was yours. My father would've never done what he did."

"Move out of the way, Tyla," Sebastian said in my mind.

While Jaret focused on Laila, I rushed over to Amelie. Her fur was covered in blood from a deep gash to her stomach. Her eyes were closed but her chest moved up and down, heart racing rapidly. "You're going to be okay," I whispered.

Sebastian snuck up the hill, followed by Finn. Jaret noticed them and spread his arms wide. "Here we are, at last." Stefan threw Laila's knife deep into the woods and dropped her to the ground so he could shift. Jaret pointed at her, his voice gravelly and dark. "You're going to wish you were dead by the time I get done with you."

He shifted and Stefan joined him, both stalking off toward Sebastian and Finn. Sebastian would have to get through them before he could get to me. My spine tingled and the hairs on my arms stood on end. The energy was so electrifyingly high, I could feel it charging everything around me. I'd never seen a battle between four lethal warriors. It was as if some unspoken countdown ensued.

I could hear Sebastian's thoughts, all jumbled together, on which steps to take and where to move. I never knew such tactics existed. Usually when I fought, I went straight in without another thought to my reactions. Maybe that was why Sebastian was the best. It was intriguing to hear him, but also terrifying to know just how skilled of a man he was. I had a lot to learn.

The time had come. Jaret lunged first and it was on. Sebastian jumped out of the way and Finn countered with a leap in Stefan's direction. Teeth snapped and the sound of ripping flesh echoed in the wind. The smell of blood was everywhere, including Sebastian's.

Laila came running over and fell to her knees beside Amelie, her throat already healing shut. She looked at Amelie's wound and placed her hands over it.

"What are you doing?"

"I'm channeling the earth's energy to heal her."

"You can do that?" I asked incredulously. I'd heard of the fae, but I'd never met one. Their magical capabilities far outstretched our own.

"Yes," she whispered. "It's part of being a fae. Since I'm part fae and part wolf, my magic is unchartered. I don't have anyone like myself to compare notes with."

The wind picked up and the ground trembled. I could feel the earth's energy seeping up through the soil, binding itself, not just Amelie, but to me as well. "What's going on?" I'd never felt anything like it.

Laila smiled, the wind blowing her long, red hair in all different directions. "It's the earth's way of saying hello to you. It's a gift."

A yelp caught my ear; it was Finn. "Oh no." I got up and raced down the hill. Finn hobbled on three of his legs, and Stefan used his momentary lack of weakness to creep up on Sebastian from behind. I could see the twinkle in Jaret's eyes as he watched Stefan close in.

If he turned to Stefan, Jaret would get him from behind. There was only one thing left to do. Taking a deep breath, I raced down the hill and shifted, my clothes tearing as they ripped off my body. Stefan was getting closer, but I was gaining on him. I jumped in the air and time stood still as I waited for my body to land on his. When I landed on his back, I bit into him and we tumbled on the ground.

"Tyla, no!"

Stefan bared his fangs and bit me in the shoulder. The pain shot through my arm and down my spine. Sebastian was too far away, but he turned and headed straight for me. *"Stop. I've got this!"*

Finn interfered first and tackled Stefan to the ground. Biting him under the neck, he held on until his body went still. Sebastian and Jaret both stopped in their tracks when Stefan went down. Jaret's eyes blazed and he howled. He was outnumbered and he knew it, but that wouldn't stop him.

Finn hung back and stood guard over me, while the final battle ensued. Their growls made the earth shake as they tore into each other. But it was easy to see who had the upper hand. Sebastian was the better fighter.

In a momentary slip of Jaret's judgment, Sebastian got a hold of one of his hind legs and latched on. Twisting and shaking, he ripped it clean off. Jaret howled in pain and tried to run away, but Sebastian tackled him and swiped his claws across his belly. Visions flashed in his mind, all of them centered on ripping Jaret apart. He wanted to make it as painful as possible. While Jaret lied on the ground, Sebastian bit into his other leg and tore it off as well.

"Tyla," Laila shouted. I looked up at the top of the hill

and saw she wasn't alone. Amelie had awakened, eyes glowing and dialed in on Jaret.

"Sebastian, stop!"

He jerked his head to the side, his white fur covered in splatters of red. *"He needs to suffer."*

"And he will. Just let Amelie deliver the final blow. She needs this."

Amelie raced down the hill, as if she was never hurt in the first place. She then circled Sebastian and Jaret, waiting for her turn to strike. A brief moment passed when Sebastian and Amelie stared at each other. I knew they couldn't speak mind to mind, but it was like there was an unspoken oath there.

When Sebastian was done, he walked away and stood beside me. *"Don't ever do what you did again. Promise me,"* he growled.

I rubbed my head against him and looked up into his glowing blue eyes. "I was worried about you. You say you refuse to lose me, but I refuse to lose you too. I'm not raising this baby on my own."

"I had it under control, Tyla. I knew Stefan was coming at me from behind. I was prepared."

"I didn't know," I said honestly.

He nudged me with his nose. "That's why you're going to let me start training you. Micah and I can help you and Amelie, and even Laila if she decides to come back with us."

The way he said Laila's name with such meaning bothered me. I knew he had been with countless women before me, but if she was his daughter, I couldn't help but be jealous of the fact. Laila joined us and stood beside Sebastian, keeping her gaze on Amelie as she continued to circle around Jaret. He yelped in pain, most likely wanting her to end it, but she let him suffer. That was exactly what I would've done. He didn't deserve a quick death.

By the smell of Jaret's blood, it wasn't going to be long before he bled out. Amelie knew this was her last chance. Instead of ripping out his throat, she shifted and grabbed a large stick off of the ground. Holding it high, she slammed it down, piercing it through his chest. He was gone in a matter of seconds.

Amelie fell to her knees, burying her head in her hands, the sound of her cries filtering back to us. Laila rushed off toward her as the rest of us shifted.

"It's over," Finn murmured.

I reached for his hand and held it. "I'm sorry you lost everyone. I didn't even get the chance to see them again."

He squeezed my hand, his amber eyes gentle. "They were happy to know you were alive, but even more than that, they were ready to end this war. For years, the Sierra Pack has hunted us down one by one. Now we don't have to fight anymore."

"True, but we lost everyone. None of our people survived."

"That's not true," he said, smiling sadly. "Three of us did."

"Where are you going to go now?" Sebastian asked.

Finn shrugged. "Don't know. I guess from here I can go anywhere."

"You can come back with us," I said.

He glanced back and forth between us, and it looked like he was considering it, but then he shook his head. "I don't think that's such a great idea just yet. Maybe one day

I'll find my way there." Pulling me into his arms, he held on tight. For years, I'd thought he was dead, and now I had to let him go all over again. "I'm going to bury my men. Be safe going home," he said.

Squeezing my eyes shut, I hugged him back and let go. "Goodbye, Finn." He shook Sebastian's hand and then took off toward his fallen wolves.

Sebastian put his arm around me and held me close. "You'll see him again, love. One way or another, your paths will cross again."

"Does that bother you?" I asked.

He shook his head. "No, but I know there's something bothering you." He nodded toward Laila.

Sighing, I glanced at her and then back to him. "When were you going to tell me?"

"Tell you what?"

"That you were her father," I blurted out. A small smile spread across his lips, then he burst out laughing. "What's so funny?"

"You are, love. I kind of enjoy this little jealous streak bubbling inside of you."

I huffed and crossed my arms across my chest. "Glad I could amuse you."

He pulled my arms apart and made me wrap them around his neck. "She's not my daughter."

I gasped. "But her eyes . . . they look exactly like yours."

He chuckled. "They do, but have you forgotten I have two brothers? Why did you assume she'd be mine?"

"I don't know," I lied. His gaze narrowed and I huffed. "Okay, fine. I know your track record with women. Out of you and your brothers, you'd be the most obvious culprit."

"And the least?" he asked.

Micah was a flirt but he wasn't as bad as Sebastian. And Zayne was a whole other story. He was more reserved and serious all the time.

Releasing a heavy sigh, he twirled one of my curls around his finger. "Just because you're not an outgoing person doesn't mean you don't know how to love."

I could feel the turmoil inside of him. "It's Zayne?" He nodded. "And he doesn't know he has a child?"

"That's something I'll have to handle as soon as we get home. I just need to make sure Laila's ready for it all."

Our homecoming was going to be the most epic yet. Sebastian and I were mated and expecting a child, we survived an epic battle from my past, I was bringing home a cousin I hadn't seen in thirty years, and I met my first wolf/fae mix—who happened to be my niece.

Our story needed to be turned into a novel. *Maybe I should try my luck at writing.*

TWENTY-SIX

SEBASTIAN

"**Y**ou don't have to do this. I know you want to get back to Tyla," Laila said.

I finished gathering the rest of the bodies and tossed them in the large hole I'd spent all morning digging. "I do, but this needed to be done." She handed me the canister of gasoline and I poured it all over the remains before tossing in a lighter. The flames burned high, then slowly died down to a steady crackling fire.

"Is it bad that I'm not sad at all?" she asked.

"No. Jaret and his wolves needed to be put down."

She looked back at the house. "I think I'm just going to leave the house the way it is. With Jaret gone, there's not much I can do with it. His name is on everything, and I don't want to have to explain how he died."

"He didn't leave *anything* to you?"

She snorted. "Are you kidding? He thought he was invincible. When I suggested he write a will, he laughed in my face."

"Cocky bastard," I grumbled.

She nodded, then met my gaze. "I have so much to tell you. It's my fault Jaret was able to find the Redwood Pack. I didn't want to tell Tyla or Amelie what I did. They'll hate me."

"What did you do?" Smoke billowed out from the ditch and with a swipe of her hand, Laila commanded the dirt to filter back into the hole as if it was never there. "How did you do that?" I asked, kneeling down to touch the dirt.

"I'm not really sure. I know it's a part of my fae heritage. From what I can gather, we all are born with a bond to either earth, fire, water, or air. As you can see, mine is with earth. Mix that in with my wolf blood, and it makes me even more powerful. I don't even know what all I'm capable of yet."

I peered down at the ground and then back to her. "So you're saying you could've dug that hole with just a snap of your fingers?"

She giggled and lifted her arms in the air. "I did tell you to wait on me. And as I remember it, you were the one who decided to start digging. I would've done it for you."

"I'll know for next time." I chuckled.

Her smile faded. "Hopefully, there won't be a next time. I've spent my whole life in war. It's all Jaret thought about." She started toward the house and I followed alongside.

The whole morning she'd spent packing up her things to take to Wyoming. Once we got inside, we carried her boxes out to the car. "So, tell me. What did you do that makes you think Amelie and Tyla will hate you?"

Body tense, she set the last box of her belongings in the back of the car and shut the trunk. "Like I said, I spent my whole life with a bunch of wolves who were seeking revenge. I was led to believe that my mother was killed by the Redwood Pack. So, many years ago, Jaret took me out to California where you all fought. The ground had absorbed the blood and I was able to extract it and use it to trace the remaining wolves. It didn't give me exact coordinates, but it was enough for Jaret to go on the hunt and track them down."

"And he killed them," I stated.

Tears filled her eyes. "I never would've done it if I'd known."

"How did you find out the truth?"

Sighing, she closed her eyes and the tears fell. "It was a year ago. I had been walking in the woods picking blackberries, when I overheard Jaret in the barn talking to Stefan. Stefan wanted to mate with me, but Jaret refused him, saying he thought it might mess with my powers." She opened her eyes and looked down at the ground. "He said my mother tried to use her magic on Vincent to fight him off, but she wasn't strong enough." She shook her head, tears springing to her eyes. "The thought of him forcing himself on her made me so sick. I stayed in my room for days trying to clear my head."

"What happened then?"

"That's when I came up with a plan on my own. I searched for something of my mother's, anything would do. There wasn't much, but I did find a small box. Inside there were a couple of her journals, written in a language I've never heard of. I figured it was some kind of fae dialect."

"Elvish. Your mother used to speak it sometimes."

"It's also where I found this." She pulled a round, pink crystal out of her pocket.

"What is that?"

"It was my mother's. She'd linked her memories to it just like I had with Amelie and the moonstone. However, this one linked to her memories, not her sight. It's also a healing stone. She must've used it during the time she was with Vincent." She closed her eyes and smiled. "It's where I first saw you and your brothers . . . and realized Vincent wasn't my father."

"Did you see her with Zayne?"

She opened her eyes and faced me, her cheeks turning red. "Maybe a little more than I should have." She laughed. "It's nice to know they loved each other though. But after I saw you and your brothers, I traced you to Wyoming, and never said anything. So one day, I flew out there and saw you and Tyla. I felt an instant connection to you. I tried looking for my father, but he wasn't there."

I shook my head. "He didn't come to the Royal pack until just recently."

"I wanted to stay, to tell you who I was, but I knew I had to get back to Jaret. He needed to be stopped and I was the only one who could do it. That's where my betrayal started with Amelie. I had found her first, and friended her behind Jaret's back. When she showed me a picture of her and Tyla, I knew it was fate. From there, I coerced Jaret to pursue Amelie instead of outright kill her. I told him it would draw Tyla in. If I could get her here, I knew I could get to you."

"What if it didn't work and he killed Amelie? What would you have done?" I asked.

Her jaw clenched. "I would've attempted to kill him myself. Luckily, I didn't have to worry about that. All I want now is to find out what I am, and if there are others like me."

As far as I knew there was no one like her, but I didn't want to tell her that. There were other fae around, but not many. "I bet Seraphina might know more about this. Let's get in the car and I'll tell you more about her."

She grabbed my arm when I started to walk around the car. "What about my father? Do you think he'll help me?"

Zayne was going to be an issue. He still harbored a grudge and I could see it getting worse when he found out about his daughter. He'd most likely think I'd kept that from him too. "He doesn't know about you, Laila," I murmured.

"I know, but I want to see him."

"Just keep in mind that it might take him some time for him to adjust. I'll introduce you to him though."

"Why did he leave my mother?" she asked as she opened the passenger door.

I shrugged. "I'm not sure. That's a question you'll have to ask him."

TWENTY-SEVEN

TYLA

"When are you going to call your parents?" Amelie asked. My phone had been dead for days and when I finally had it charged, there were so many missed calls I lost count.

I taped up another box and sat down on her bed. "I'll call in a minute. Right now I'm just worried about you. You've been quiet since we got back."

She boxed up her books and sat down with me. "I'm fine, I promise. I just miss my parents more than anything. But I feel free now that Jaret's gone."

"Do you miss him?"

She shrugged. "Only the person I thought he was. When we'd first met, he'd been so charming and loving. It's crazy how people can hide who they truly are."

"One day, you'll find a man who makes you happy. There are a lot of eligible bachelors in Wyoming," I said with a wink.

Laughing, she hit me across the head with a pillow.

"Don't you dare try to set me up with anyone right away. I'm not ready for all that crap."

I smiled and took the pillow. "I won't. But you seriously could meet your true mate out there. I know I did."

"And you said his brothers look just like him?" she asked.

"Yep, and you'll meet them soon." My phone started to ring and I looked down at it. "I should probably answer that." Taking a deep breath, I answered the call. "Hey, what's up?"

"What's *up*? That's all you have to say to me?" my mother exclaimed.

"Umm . . . I love you?" I added, stifling a laugh. Amelie smiled and shook her head.

"Why haven't you returned my calls? We've been worried sick about you."

I laid back on the bed. "It's been a hard couple of days."

"What happened?"

I glanced over at Amelie. "Well, we found Amelie, but we also happened to find the Sierra Pack—they were the ones who had her. Needless to say, we were captured, tortured, and a battle ensued, but at least now it's over for good."

She gasped. "Was anyone hurt? Tell me everything."

My eyes burned as I went through the whole spiel, telling her everything from start to finish.

"Oh my God, Tyla. Why didn't you call for help? We would've been out there as fast as we could."

"There was no time, Momma."

"And Finn?" she asked.

"He's alive, but he left. I don't know where to. I tried to get him to join our pack, but he wasn't ready for that."

She repeated everything I'd just said to my father and he snatched the phone away from her. She huffed, demanding for the phone back but he refused. "Baby, are you okay?"

"I'm fine, Dad. We'll be home in a couple of days. We're packing up Amelie's stuff now and starting the drive back in the morning."

"Where's Sebastian?"

I heard the car pull into the driveway and smiled. "He's here. I'll call you when we're almost home so you can get everyone together. There's so much I need to tell you all."

"Just be careful coming home."

My mother hollered that she wanted to talk to Amelie and ended up grabbing the phone. "I want to talk to her," she demanded.

Amelie folded the shirt she was holding, threw it in her suitcase, and held out her hand with a smile. "Even without my wolf hearing, I could hear her all the way across the room," she whispered low. I held out the phone and she took it. "Aunt Soph!" she squealed.

"Tyla?" Sebastian called out from down below, his foot-steps coming up the stairs. I waved at Amelie and met him out in the hallway.

He pulled me into his arms and kissed me. "How'd it go today?"

"Um," I glanced at all the boxes in the hallway, "we're going to need a moving truck to haul this shit to Wyoming."

Chuckling, he lifted me up and carried me into the guest bedroom we'd be using for the night. We had just one more day before we headed home. "We can get some of the other pack members to come out and help with that. I'm just ready to get you home."

He laid me on the bed and I snuggled into his side. It was the first time we'd been able to really hold each other since the fight. "What are we going to do when we get there, you know, now that we're mated?"

His fingers drifted to the hem of my shirt, tickling my skin. "That's up to you, love. I'd like for you to move in with me. We can always sell your house."

Amelie and Laila could be heard talking quietly downstairs, and then an idea popped in my mind. "I might see if Amelie and Laila want to live there. I don't particularly want them staying with us, and I know they aren't going to want to live with my parents."

Sebastian kissed my head. "That's a great idea. I'm sure they'll appreciate it." He moved over and turned me onto my back, placing his hand on my stomach. "I don't know what I would've done if I'd lost you both."

I covered his hand with mine. "You don't have to worry about that. I'm right here and so is . . ." I stopped and looked down at my stomach, "our son or daughter."

He lifted my shirt and kissed my belly. "I bet it's a girl. I want her to have your curls."

"And your eyes," I added. "But I wonder if she'll be a gray or white wolf?"

"Not sure, but we'll get to find out soon enough," he said, lifting my shirt higher. Making his way up my stomach, his lips landed on my breasts.

"What are you doing?"

Reaching behind me, he unclasped my bra and slid it

up, closing his lips over a taut nipple. I sucked in a breath and trembled. "I'm going to make love to my mate," he whispered low.

"What about Amelie and Laila?"

He kissed his way up my neck and chuckled in my ear. "They're big girls, they can handle it. And if they don't want to, the outdoors is wide and vast."

I would've normally protested, but I needed him right then and there. After discarding our clothes, Sebastian crawled up my body, smirking in a way that made my body tighten. Closing his lips over mine, he reached down to slip a finger inside me. As soon as his fingers found me wet, he growled deep in his chest.

"You're killing me."

I bit my lip and smiled. "You know what to do."

He stretched my legs wider as he got into position. Licking his hand, he rubbed himself and then pressed his tip against my opening. Gently, he pushed inside. I loved how he filled me. Holding my hands above my head, he made love to me while keeping eye contact. My body trembled and I could feel my orgasm building. He rocked his hips more vigorously, his fingers tightening around mine.

"I love you," his voice echoed in my mind, making me smile.

My whole body tightened and I moaned. *"I love you too."*

Digging my nails into the back of his hands, I screamed out his name as he released inside me. Still connected, Sebastian let go of my hands and kissed me, his lips warm and smooth. "You have no idea how amazing that felt."

"I know what would feel even more amazing," I whispered. I thought about what I wanted in my mind.

He bit his lip and smiled. "You sure that's what you want?"

Tilting my head to the side, I blew out a shaky breath. "Yes." I was scared about us simultaneously taking each other's blood, for fear of what I'd see in our vision. But if we didn't do it, I'd always wonder. "I want to taste you too," I murmured. He licked his lips and slowly edged closer to me, his mouth on my neck. Breathing me in, I felt his fangs press against my skin. *"I'm ready, Sebastian."*

His teeth sank into my neck, as my own found purchase in his shoulder; the sweet taste of his blood flowing down my throat. Everything around us changed and we were thrust into a magical world of swirling mist. Only this time, it was a real place, and Sebastian was right beside me.

"This is weird," I said, glancing around the field. There were mountains everywhere, but we weren't in Wyoming. "Where are we?"

Sebastian intertwined his fingers with mine, a twinkle in his eyes. "Canada, my home." He pulled me with him and pointed at a house in the distance. "That's my house down there, or what used to be it. It's changed so much. I haven't seen it in so long."

We walk toward it and I could feel the cool breeze sweeping across the landscape. "It's beautiful here," I said in awe. If I didn't have my family in Wyoming, I'd move there in a heartbeat.

Sebastian nodded and I couldn't help but notice the fascination on his face. He'd lived his life protecting others. It made me wonder if he missed the kind of life he could've had, one of freedom.

His gaze met mine. "I had freedom, love. Freedom is choice, and I chose to protect my kind. It was what I wanted to do. In the end, it brought me to you. I wouldn't change a thing."

"Nothing?"

He leaned over and kissed me. "Nothing."

The closer we got to the house, the faster my heart raced. "What do you think we'll find in there?"

That was when I heard it . . . laughing. We were almost to the house when the door burst open and an older version of me came running out. I barely recognized myself. My skin was wrinkled and my long hair had lost its blonde in favor of a bright white.

"Holy shit, that's me," I whispered.

Sebastian chuckled. "And you can still move too."

I smacked him on the arm. "Let's see how you catch up to me, old man. You're a lot older than me."

The old me held up her hand to shield the sun from her eyes, her chest rising and falling with her rapid breaths. "Sebastian? Where are you, old man?"

I burst out laughing. "She actually said it. This is crazy. I wonder where you're at."

Sebastian smiled and pulled me close. "Don't worry, I'm coming." I searched around the land, not finding him anywhere.

"Don't tell me you're scared?" The old me laughed. She started walking back to the house and that was when I saw a blur out of the corner of my eye. The old Sebastian came out of nowhere and lunged for her, taking her down to the ground. She laughed as they rolled down the hill.

Sebastian and I rushed down after them and found them holding each other in the grass, still laughing.

"You're still as beautiful as ever," Sebastian murmured.

I finally got a good look at the old Sebastian and my heart raced. His hair was white with wisps of dark gray, but no amount of wrinkles could take away the handsomeness of his face or the brightness of his blue eyes.

"And you're still sexy as hell," I replied back with a wink.

The old us started to kiss and when they stopped, they just stared into each other's eyes. It felt strange spying on myself many years from now, but it gave me the closure I needed. We had a chance to live a long, peaceful life together.

"Do you think all visions will be like this?" I asked.

He brushed the hair off my face. "I don't know, but I look forward to finding out."

TWENTY-EIGHT

TYLA

It had taken us two full days to make the trek from North Carolina to Wyoming. We'd stopped along the way to rest, but for the most part, we'd stayed on the road. I was way past ready to get home.

Laila had decided to stay in the truck and keep her presence hidden until we were able to introduce her. She thought that if everyone could sense her, it'd take away from the family reunion. I think it was because she wanted to stay hidden longer. I knew she was nervous about joining a new pack.

We turned down my parents' street and there were cars lined up in their driveway. My mother burst out of the house and waved as we pulled in, followed by my father.

"Here we go," I said, giving Sebastian a please-help-me look.

Amelie parked behind us and burst out of the truck, jumping into their arms. My mother cried and ran her hands all over Amelie's face. Bailey, Ryker, Micah, and Seraphina joined them on the porch and as soon as Sebastian and I stepped out, it was as if the whole world stopped. They all looked at us and froze.

Sebastian put his arm around me and leaned down, whispering in my ear. "I think the cat's out of the bag."

I snickered. "I do wish they would say something."

Upon hearing this, my mother squealed and Amelie had to jump out of the way before getting trampled as she raced down the steps. My father beamed and nodded in approval.

Clasping my face in her hands, my mother glanced back and forth, from me to Sebastian. I'd never seen her so happy. "You were right when you said you had a lot to tell me. I can't believe you actually did it! Your father and I were afraid you'd let your hard head get in the way."

Sebastian tried to hide his chuckle and failed. "Thanks, Mom," I grumbled.

My father joined us and shook Sebastian's hand. "Thanks for bringing her home safely, son."

Sebastian beamed and slapped him on the shoulder. "Trust me, it wasn't easy."

"Hey," I snapped, elbowing him in the side.

Bailey rushed down to us and flung her arms around me, whispering in my ear. "I knew you wouldn't let me down. I don't think I've ever seen him smile so much, or you for that matter."

"It's because I haven't," I whispered back. I winked at Sebastian over her shoulder and he smiled.

She then let me go and wrapped her arms around Sebastian, kissing him on the cheek. "The ladies are going to be so upset when they see you're taken."

I snorted. "If they have a problem with that, I'll be more than happy to deal with each of them on a one to one basis."

Amelie giggled. "What are you going to do, waddle after them?"

Sebastian's arm tightened around me and I froze at her comment. My mother glanced at Amelie and then to me, clearly thinking she missed something.

Seraphina was the one who walked up to me and touched my stomach. "Well, what do you know?" She beamed at Sebastian. "This is amazing news. I knew you two would find your way to each other."

My mother screamed out in joy and I laughed. Micah and Ryker pulled Sebastian away, congratulating him, while the girls surrounded me. "I'm going to be a grandma," my mother cried. "I never thought this day would come."

I rolled my eyes. "Thanks, Mom."

She placed her hands on my stomach and squatted low, telling the baby what all they were going to do together. When she stood, her brows furrowed. "Wait a second. How did you find out you were pregnant so fast? If you and Sebastian just mated, there's no way you'd know without Seraphina's help."

Amelie glanced at the car and then to me and Sebastian. I nodded at her and she went to the car, opening the door. Laila unleashed her power and the whole world stood still for the second time that day.

Sebastian joined us and motioned for the guys to follow him. When Laila stepped out of the truck, the only sound to be heard was that of the snow's soft pitter-patter as it landed on the ground. I specifically watched for Micah's reaction. He stared at Laila as if she was a ghost.

Micah grabbed Sebastian's arm. "What's going on, brother?"

"I'll tell you in just a minute. Hang tight," he whispered. Walking over to Laila, Sebastian stood beside her. "Everyone, this is Laila. She's going to be joining our pack."

Bailey and Ryker smiled and introduced themselves, while my mother flanked me on the right and Micah and Seraphina on the left. "What is she?" my mother asked.

"It's a long story," I told her. "Why don't you take Amelie and go inside? Sebastian and I need to talk to Micah and Seraphina."

My parents took my advice and led Amelie inside, followed by Bailey and Ryker. Sebastian whispered something to Laila and her gaze lifted to Micah who couldn't tear his eyes away from her.

"I think your brother's in shock," I said.

Sebastian looked at me and then at Micah. *"I do believe you're right. I want to make sure he keeps this secret to himself until I can tell Zayne."* He and Laila stepped up to us and she smiled at them. "Seraphina, Micah, this is Laila," Sebastian said.

Laila focused on Micah first, her gaze twinkling as she held out her hand. "I'm happy to finally meet you. Sebastian's told me all about you."

Micah took her hand. "You look . . ."

"Like my mother, I know. I can only imagine what you must be thinking right now."

"Just a little shocked is all." He let her hand go and turned to Sebastian. "I'd like to know what's going on."

Sebastian nodded. "Give us a second and I'll tell you everything." He turned Laila to Seraphina. "Laila, Seraphina is one of our pack elders. I'm hoping she'll be able to help guide you through some of your powers."

Seraphina grabbed her hand and held it. "It's a pleasure to meet you, child. I must say, you have me very intrigued. Your power is something I've never felt."

"I could say the same for you," she replied back. "If you don't mind, I'd love to ask you some questions. There is so much I don't understand."

Seraphina linked her arm with hers. "I'd be happy to help in any way I can. Why don't we take a walk?" Laila looked to Sebastian for approval and he nodded. Once they walked off, he turned his focus to Micah.

Micah's jaw tensed. "She looks just like Alina."

Sighing, Sebastian placed a hand on his shoulder. "There's a reason for that. Laila's her daughter. I didn't know she even existed until we found her in North Carolina a few days ago. She has been living with the Sierra Pack, thinking she was one of them. Her fae blood made it hard for others to differentiate what she actually was. I'm assuming that's what kept her alive all these years. They would've killed her if they'd known she wasn't one of them."

Closing his eyes, he ran a hand through his hair. "She's an Arctic, brother. I can sense our kind from a mile away." He opened his eyes and it was obvious he knew.

"She's more than just your kind," Sebastian murmured. "She's your niece."

He looked up at the sky and sighed. "When are you going to tell Zayne?"

Sebastian glanced at me, his gaze sad and full of pain. "As soon as Laila's ready. I just needed you to keep this to yourself until I got that chance to talk to him. Besides, you'll need to be there for him once he finds out."

Micah placed a hand on his shoulder. "I'll be there. I

can't imagine what it's going to be like for him. She looks so much like her mother. But for so long, all we've had were each other. It's nice to know our family is growing." He turned to me. "I guess this means no more sparring?"

I shook my head. "Not for a while, but I want Amelie and Laila to learn how to fight. You and Sebastian would make great teachers."

He nodded. "I'll be more than happy to. I just hope once Sebastian talks to Zayne, he'll be alive to help." He gave a sad smile and walked toward the house, leaving Sebastian and I alone in the yard.

"Is it really going to be that bad?" I asked.

"I'm not sure. I guess we'll find out tomorrow."

"Do you want me to come with you?"

Pulling me into his arms, he held me tight. I breathed him in and laid my head on his chest. "It's probably best you don't. It's something I need to do on my own. But right now, I want to take you to our home. I'm ready to spend the night alone with my mate."

TWENTY-NINE

SEBASTIAN

The next morning, after a tour of my house, Tyla had been going from room to room, trying to figure out which one would be perfect for the baby. Her hair was a tangled mess and she was wearing one of my button down shirts, looking sexier than ever. How the hell had I gotten so lucky?

"I think this one will be perfect for the baby's room," Tyla suggested. The room was empty, except for a desk I'd never used. But it had one of the best views of the mountain range in the house. "What do you think? We could paint the walls and put the crib here," she said, pointing at a corner in the room. "That way, she can see the mountains when she wakes up."

"She?"

Tyla giggled. "It's better than calling the baby an *it*. We'll find out soon enough what we're having. Maybe Laila will be able to tell us."

"Speaking of Laila, I'm going to run by your old house and talk to her. I want to know what Seraphina said. Plus, I want to make sure she's ready for me to tell my brother. If she gives me the go, I'm heading over to his place this afternoon." I didn't look forward to confronting my brother, but it had to be done.

Tyla nodded and wrapped her arms around my neck. "You can do this. And you're right, it needs to be done before word gets to him that a mysterious fae/wolf has joined our ranks. It'll only add to his resentment."

"And that's what I want to avoid." I squeezed her tight, then let go, making my way to the door. "What are you going to do today?" I asked.

"I want to go to the ranch and see Blake. I haven't talked to him since we were in North Carolina. He's probably wondering if I'm ever coming back."

"Are you still planning on working? You know you don't have to."

She shrugged. "I'll probably take a break while I'm pregnant, but once the baby is born, I'd like to get back to horse training. I enjoy it."

Her passion was what drove me to her in the first place. She was a fighter with a strong spirit. "It's your choice," I replied. "You're free to do whatever you want."

She bit her lip. "You might regret saying that. Next thing you know, you'll come home and these walls will be bright pink."

"Whatever you want, love."

Her mouth gaped. "I think I need to get pregnant more often, if it's going to be like this."

"I'll be happy to oblige. I've always wanted a big family." I looked down at my phone and sighed. "But right now I have to go. I'll see you this afternoon."

She blew me a kiss and I left. Her old house wasn't far from mine and when I pulled up into the driveway, Amelie and Laila were on the front porch drinking hot chocolate. "Don't you have unpacking to do?" I asked.

They looked at each other and smiled. "We thought we'd take a break," Amelie said.

Laila snorted and pointed at her. "*She* needed to take a break. *I'm* already done. But then again, I didn't bring a truck full of boxes."

Amelie rolled her eyes. "I've been packing up some of Tyla's things too. I'm sure she'll want them."

I nodded. "I'll take some of it home with me today. Thank you for doing that. Is there anything either of you need?"

They shook their heads and Amelie answered. "I think we're good. The house is amazing. I can see why Tyla wanted to live here." She finished up her drink and stood. "I know you two want to talk, so I'll go inside to give you some privacy."

"Thanks, Amelie," I said. She waved and shut the door behind her.

I took her seat beside Laila and looked out at the mountains. "You okay?" I asked.

"I'm fine. Actually, I'm better than ever now that I've talked to Seraphina."

I turned to her. "What all did you discuss?"

She set her cup down and faced me, folding her legs underneath her in the chair. "Lots of stuff. She said she's met other fae over the years and even learned some of their language. It's Elvish, just like you'd said. She's going to try and help me translate my mother's journals."

"That's great. Does she know anything else about your people? The only other thing I know is that the fae aren't from our world. They come from—"

"The Land of the Fae," she finished. "Yes, Seraphina told me that. I can't seem to comprehend that my mother wasn't a part of this planet. It's weird even thinking about it."

"Zayne might know more about her home than I do, since he was closest to your mother."

Sighing, she averted her gaze. "When are you going to see him?"

"As soon as I leave here, if that's okay with you. I want to talk to him before introductions are made."

She nodded. "I'm ready for it to happen. I've been dying to meet him since I found out the truth. Other than you and Micah, he's my only family left. Will it hurt him to see me? I know I look just like my mother, except for my eyes."

"I'm not going to lie, it'll probably bring back the pain of her loss when he sees you, but it'll pass. It might take some time, but I know he'll love you the moment you walk through his door. You're his daughter, Laila, his blood. There's nothing more important than that."

She squeezed my hand and let it go. "I hope you're right. Make sure to call me when you're done. I'll be sitting on the edge of my seat."

We said our goodbyes and I went to my car, heading on my way. Zayne's house was tucked back farther into the woods. He liked it that way, so he could have his solitude. He was older than me and Micah, but not by much. We all looked the same with our whitish-blond hair and blue eyes.

We'd always been mistaken for triplets, even though there were considerable differences to our appearances, and our personalities were as diverse as they could be.

When I pulled into Zayne's driveway, I could sense Colin was there with him. The door was cracked open, so I made my way inside. They were in Zayne's drawing room, where he worked on his building sketches. Both he and Colin designed houses for a living.

They were deep in thought, both on each side of the massive sketch when I knocked on the door. "Knock, knock," I said.

"Sebastian," Zayne announced, not even lifting his head to acknowledge me. "I see you're back in town."

Colin stood and extended his hand. "Bailey called me last night and told me everything. Looks like you got mixed up in a pack war. Glad to see you and Tyla made it back safely."

"Thanks, man," I said, taking his hand.

"And congrats on the baby. You must've been afraid she'd choose me when you got back home," he teased, letting my hand go. Zayne lifted his head, eyes wide. Colin must not have told him.

Chuckling, I slapped Colin on the shoulder. "Not a chance in hell, Storm."

"Well, I'll be damned," Zayne said, getting to his feet. "I never thought I'd see the day you'd be mated." A small smile spread across his face. He was genuinely happy for me. Too bad he wouldn't be for long. He held out his hand and I took it. "I'm happy for you, brother. But what's this I've heard about a pack war? I thought you were just going to find Tyla's family?"

I shook his hand and let go. "That was the plan, but it ended up being more in depth than that. I'd like to tell you a little more about it, if you have time."

"Sure. But first, I want you to see what I've been working on. Take a look at this," he said, waving me toward his drawing table.

"What am I looking at here?" I asked, viewing the sketches. There were three different designs, all completely different.

"We've been working on these designs for a client and we're showing them to him next week. Which one do you like? I don't know which one to push."

"Where is it going to be built?"

"Out in Wilson. This guy's from upstate New York, trying to turn himself into a cowboy. He wants something rustic, yet upscale. He has a really good view of the mountains on this side of the house," he said, pointing to the west side of the drawings.

I studied the diagrams and chose the one with the best layout. "This one has more open space in the main room. If this guy is as pretentious as he sounds, he'll be focused more on the large kitchen and living room to impress his visitors. That's what everyone will see first."

"See?" Colin said. "That's exactly what I said." He nudged me in the arm. "But what do we know?"

We both chuckled and Zayne shook his head. "Keep it up, you two. I'm not afraid to kick both of your asses."

"Like you could, old man," Colin countered. He looked over at the clock. "Ah shit, I have to go. Got a meeting with a potential client." He rushed out of the room.

"Let me know how it goes," Zayne shouted after him.

He sat back down and focused on his sketches. "So, tell me what happened. Were you in danger?"

Chuckling, I sat down in the seat across from him. "You have no idea." I got into the details, starting with Tyla's aunt and uncle, and ending with the enemy pack who'd lured us into their trap.

Brows furrowed, he stared at me. "But why would they want to lure *you* in? How were you connected to all of this?"

"Because in one hell of a coincidence, I'd killed their alpha. They've been hunting me for thirty years."

Eyes flashing, Zayne stiffened, his hands clenching into tight fists. "Who?"

"I think you know who." He pushed his chair away from the desk and stood, the chair falling to the ground, his anger permeating the room. "His son was who took Amelie. He planned on mating with Tyla to repeat exactly what his father had done."

"Did you kill him?" he growled.

"He's dead, along with the rest of the Sierra Pack. There were no survivors."

"Good." He huffed and ran a hand through his hair. When he finally collected himself, he picked up his chair and set it upright. I waited for him to look at me, but he sat back at his desk and reached for his drawing pencils.

"We need to end this feud, brother. I know keeping you in the dark all those years ago was a mistake, but I only did it to protect you. Attacking that pack in a fit of rage would've cost you your life. I couldn't have saved you."

"I wouldn't have cared," he replied, his gaze full of pain. "My life was forfeit once she was gone. I'm still not over her death. It haunts me every day. If I'd just left Canada sooner to get her, it wouldn't have happened. I never would've . . ." He stopped and bit his lip.

"Never would've what?" I asked.

He waved it off. "It doesn't matter anymore. What's done is done. We can't change a goddamned thing."

"No, but we can make it better. I need you to forgive me, brother. What I did was out of love for you. I miss Alina too. She wouldn't want to see us like this."

Setting his pencil down, Zayne ran a hand over his face. "You're right, she wouldn't. That's why I can forgive you now. But it still doesn't take away the pain. I've lived with nothing but regret for the past thirty years."

"So have I," I said truthfully. "I understand now why you hated me so much for taking away your revenge."

He sighed. "I don't hate you, Sebastian. You're my brother." He held out his hand. "All is forgiven."

Taking his hand, I squeezed it tight. "Thank you, I'll take it. But unfortunately, I'm not done with what I have to say."

"There's more?"

Nodding, I licked my dry lips. "First, I need to ask you a question." He stared at me, waiting. "Did you ever mate with Alina on the full moon?"

Gaze narrowed, he lifted his chin. "Why are you asking that?"

"Please just answer the question," I insisted.

"I loved her, Sebastian. We spent many nights together until I was called back to Canada." My heart raced and he could hear it. "What are you not telling me? Why do you want to know this information?"

I kept my gaze on his, eyes never wavering. The last thing I wanted was to bring him more pain, but I had to believe Laila would be what he needed to heal. "There was a child," I said, releasing a heavy sigh.

His breath caught. "What do you mean there was a child?"

"Alina was pregnant when Vincent took her for his mate. The girl's name is Laila, and she was the one who helped us fight the Sierra Pack."

Jaw clenching, his whole body shook. "What the fuck are you saying Sebastian? Just spit it out."

"I'm saying that Laila is your daughter. I didn't know she was yours until I saw her for the first time. However, she's known about us for a while now. It was her plan all along to get me and Tyla out there to help her. It was the only way to end the Sierra Pack."

His face turned red and he sucked in a breath, his eyes growing wet. "Does she know I'm her father?"

I nodded. "She found out through some of Alina's belongings. There was a stone with some of her memories on it. When Laila touched it, she was able to see all of us, including you."

"Where is she now?" he asked. I could hear the desperation in his voice; he was worried about her.

"She's staying at Tyla's house. And she wants to meet you."

He huffed. "What am I supposed to say to her? 'Hi, I'm your father. Sorry I failed you and your mother.'"

"No, you didn't," I growled. "She doesn't blame you for what happened. She's lost, and needs your help. You're her only family, her only connection to her mother. She needs you, and I believe you need her too."

He dropped his head to his desk, crying silently.

I didn't want to leave him, but I knew he needed to be alone. My heart hurt for him and I couldn't begin to imagine what he must be feeling. I started for the door and stopped. "I know this is a lot to take in, but I'll be bringing her over here tomorrow morning. I don't think I'd be able to keep her away any longer than that if I tried." I walked out and breathed a sigh of relief.

"It's done," I said to Tyla.

"And you're still alive? I take it everything went okay?"

"I'm not sure yet. I guess we'll see when tomorrow comes.

THIRTY

I sat in Laila's room and watched her change into a million different outfits. "I don't think he's going to care what you wear," I said.

She held up a dark, navy sweater to her chest and looked in the mirror. "I just want him to like me."

"He's your father. Of course he's going to like you."

She tossed the sweater onto the bed and grabbed a cream colored one, slipping it over her head. "I've rehearsed what I was going to say over and over last night, and none of it sounds good. Knowing me, I'll walk right up to him and forget my name. It's not every day you meet your father."

I pulled her hair out from underneath the sweater and faced her. "You'll do fine, I promise. Now let's get going."

Taking a deep breath, she closed her eyes and nodded. "I can do this."

We walked out of her room and met Sebastian and Amelie in the living room. Amelie gave her a hug and a pep talk. I loved how close they had become. Sebastian started for the door. "All right, ladies, let's get this over with."

Amelie stayed home, while Sebastian and I drove Laila to Zayne's. She tapped her fingers against the seat and her leg bounced up and down, making the car shake. When we pulled up to Zayne's, I thought she was going to pass out from hyperventilating.

"What am I going to do if he doesn't want to see me?" she asked nervously.

Sebastian glanced at her in the rearview mirror. "He does. He's just afraid you think he failed you. He feels ashamed for not being there to protect you."

"But he didn't know I existed. I don't blame him for that."

"Then maybe you should tell him so," Sebastian suggested.

We all got out of the car and started for the front door. Sebastian walked inside and I stayed beside Laila, keeping a hand wrapped around her arm. I didn't want her to bolt.

"Zayne?" Sebastian called.

There was no sound in the house. In fact, I couldn't feel anyone's presence around at all. Surely, Zayne didn't up and leave, knowing very well Laila was coming over to see him. If he did, it was a dick move. Hopefully, Sebastian would kick his ass if that was the case.

"Don't worry, love. If he's not here, I'll be doing more than kicking his ass."

"He's not here, is he?" Laila said, her voice sounding deflated.

My heart ached for her. I put my arm around her and squeezed her shoulder. "We'll find him. He has to be here somewhere."

Sebastian walked out the back door and froze. *"He's out here, love. Bring Laila."*

"Sebastian says he's outside," I whispered.

She sucked in a breath and nodded. "I'm ready."

I walked with her through the door and stopped by Sebastian's side. I followed his gaze across the field to where Zayne stood with his back to us. "Should we walk her out there?" I questioned. I felt like a mother hen protecting one of her chicks.

Laila couldn't take her eyes away from Zayne. "No," she said, lifting her chin. "I want to do this on my own."

"Are you sure?" Sebastian asked.

She nodded. "I think it'll be better this way. Unless he won't want to talk to me, that is."

I stepped in front of her. "He'd be stupid if he doesn't. I have faith in you, Laila. You can do this." She hugged me and Sebastian before walking out into the field, her steps slow and timid.

My heart pounded with each of her steps. "I wish I knew what was going to happen," I whispered.

Sebastian sighed. "Me too. We should probably leave for a little while to give them privacy. I know my brother. If he thinks we're close, he'll be on guard. He doesn't like to show emotion."

"Just like another Lyall I know," I teased.

Taking my hand, he led me through the house and out to the car. "I was only like that at the beginning. You don't have to worry about that now."

"I know, babe." He opened the car door for me and I got in. "Laila won't be mad that we left her will she?"

"I don't think they'll be done anytime soon." He shut

my door and got behind the wheel. "Is there anything you want to do?"

My insides tightened and I squeezed my legs shut. Ever since I'd found out I was pregnant, it was as if my whole body was in heat. I loved it and I knew Sebastian did too.

"I think we have plenty of time for that," he said, reading my mind.

We started on our way home and I closed my eyes, remembering our last vision. It had been a beautiful place. I opened my eyes and turned to him. "How about once everything settles down, we go to Canada? I want to see your home, where you grew up. I want to be where we were in the vision."

Taking my hand, he lifted it to his lips. "I'll take you anywhere you want to go. I know you'll love it there. There's so much I can show you. It'll be nice to see it again."

"Then it's a date. I want to go as soon as we can. After everything we've been through, we need a vacation."

He chuckled. "That's for damn sure."

THIRTY-ONE

LAILA

My heart pounded the closer I got to him, and his beat even harder. I was still staring at his back and I longed to see his face. I'd seen it in my mother's stone, but that wasn't good enough. I wanted to run and jump in his arms; to tell him how, even though I didn't know him, I loved him. Maybe it was stupid of me to think we could have a normal relationship. But I had to try.

Sebastian accepted me as his niece. If all else failed, I'd have him and Tyla. Swallowing hard, I closed the distance, leaving only three feet between us. I didn't know if I should say the first word or wait for him to turn around. I'd heard of the Lyall stubbornness and figured it was probably best if I made the first move.

"Hi," I said, my voice just above a whisper. He stiffened and didn't turn around. "My name is Laila, but I'm sure you already know that by now." Still, I waited for him to turn around and he didn't. It didn't matter though, as long as I said what I had to say. "I know all of this has come as a shock to you. Believe me, it was the same for me when I found out. I just want you to know I don't blame you for not knowing. How could you? Nobody knew, other than my mother, but by then it was too late."

His shoulders hunched and his head fell, breaking my heart. "Please talk to me," I pleaded. When he didn't, I held back my tears. I remembered what it had been like on the day I'd found out the truth. It had taken me some time too. "There's something I want to give you. It was my mother's." In my hand, I held a black, velvet bag that kept her pink stone safe. I set it on the ground behind him and stepped back.

"I don't know if you ever saw her with it, but it's her rose quartz. She spelled it to capture her memories. It's where I saw you for the first time." I took another step back, hoping he'd face me. "If you ever want to find me, I'll be at Tyla's. She was nice enough to let me stay at her place." For another few seconds, I waited, before realizing nothing was going to come of it. My throat closed up tight. I didn't think I could speak, even if I wanted to.

Turning on my heel, I pulled out my phone and started to text Sebastian but thought better of it and put it away. He'd only get pissed if he found out my father ignored me, and probably start some big fight.

"Wait," my father's voice called out. Heart pounding, I turned around quickly. He glanced down at the velvet bag and picked it up, keeping his gaze on it. When he looked inside, a sad smile spread across his cheeks. "I gave this to her when we were kids. She used to carry it around everywhere. I found it in the creek by my house."

My moonstone was in my pocket and I pulled it out. "I must take after her then. I always carry mine with me too."

He took a deep breath and lifted his gaze to mine. Eyes wide, he stared at me. "You look just like her," his voice cracked, tears threatening to spill down his cheeks.

I turned my head. "I know it pains you to look at me. If it's too much, I'll understand if you don't want to see me again."

He took a step forward, and then another, until he was right in front of me. His fingers lifted my chin and I lost the battle with my tears. "Don't ever think that, Laila. Seeing you makes me miss your mother more, sure. But now I have a piece of her here with me. I just wish you knew how much I hate myself right now."

"Why did you leave?" I asked.

His fingers fell from my chin and I could feel his anger. "Being a protector has always been my way of life. I knew that when the time came, I'd have to make a choice. I was prepared to defy my pack to be with her. And so, the night after your mother and I were together, I left to go back to Canada. I was to be back in a couple of weeks, but it ended up being closer to a month. When I showed up at her house, she was gone. There wasn't a trace of her anywhere."

"Vincent," I growled.

He nodded. "But I didn't know that at the time. I searched and searched for her, and there was nothing. I figured she'd gone back to the Land of the Fae. She'd always gone back there for visits because she loved it. In fact, the only reason she'd stayed on Earth was because of me."

He turned the stone over in his hand and rubbed it between his finger and thumb. "After months and months of looking, I went back to Canada to fulfill my duty as a protector. Sebastian and Micah still had time to explore the world and it was Sebastian who found out she had been killed by Vincent. Only, he didn't tell me until *after* he'd already killed him."

"And you were mad because it was your right to do it yourself," I added.

"I loved her, Laila. For the past thirty years, I've lived in a darkness I can't seem to find my way out of. And now there's you, a daughter I had no clue existed. The thought of what you went through while being with those monsters plagues me. And again, my brother was the one who ended them, when it should've been me."

I shook my head. "Life isn't all about vengeance. But if it makes it any easier, the Sierra Pack never hurt me. They knew they couldn't. I was actually the one who turned on them and delivered death to their door. Sebastian and Amelie helped, but it was my doing. Take comfort in knowing that it was me who did it as well. I'm a part of you which means you were there too."

He brushed a finger across my cheek. "Wise beyond your years."

"I must take after my father in that respect." He chuckled and it made me smile. "I don't know much about my mother and I'm hoping you can help me with that. I was left with only a few of her memories, and a couple journals written in Elvish that I can't translate."

"I guess that means you'll need my help." He smirked.

I gasped. "You know Elvish?"

He nodded. "Your mother taught me. I'll help you with anything you need."

Jumping in his arms, I didn't care if it was overstepping my boundaries or not. I was surprised when he wrapped his arms around my waist. "I feel like I've waited an eternity for this one moment."

"So have I, my dear. And I promise I won't let you down."

For once in my life, I finally felt like I belonged.

THIRTY-TWO

TYLA

THREE MONTHS LATER

"So you're quitting on me, eh?" Blake called, joining me at the fence.

I rolled my eyes. "I'm not quitting. I'm just taking a leave of absence, I think. I'm not sure yet. Besides, I found a replacement. You can't complain too much."

Amelie rode around the field on Nightshade, Blake's black stallion. She was just as good with horses as I was. Blake stood beside me—leaning his elbows over the fence—watching her with a skeptical eye. "I don't know if she's as good as you, but I'll see what she's got. She can start on Monday."

I waved Amelie in and she trotted over. "Thanks, Boss. I think this is exactly what she needs."

Smiling, he nudged me in the shoulder. "No problem. Just please consider coming back after the baby's born. I don't know what I'll do without you."

"I thought you said you could handle this place on your own?" I teased.

He chuckled. "I can, but you're my friend. I've kind of

gotten used to you being around. Just promise me you'll think about it."

"I promise."

"Hey, before I forget, I need to catch up with Sebastian. Maybe we can meet at the bar tomorrow night? There's something I need his help on."

"Of course, I'm sure he'll be happy to help." He patted me on the back and walked back toward the barn. Amelie finally made it over to me and I rubbed Nightshade's muzzle. "Looks like you have a job come Monday," I told her excitedly.

She beamed. "Thank you, Tyla. I won't let you down."

"I know you won't. But let's put this big boy back in his stall for the night, so I can get home." I helped her put Nightshade back and showed her around the barn. There were two new horses she'd have to help train and I knew she could do it.

Once I dropped her off, I hurried home and rushed to the kitchen. I was craving grapes. Morning sickness didn't bother shifters, but the cravings were ridiculous. One day, I'd want grapes, the next, Brussel sprouts, and so on. My weirdest craving had been tuna and chocolate syrup sandwiches.

I grabbed a handful of grapes and popped them into my mouth, one after the other. "Sebastian?" I called.

"Up here."

What was he doing in the nursery? I walked up the stairs but couldn't see him because the door was closed. I opened it up and gasped when the room came into view. The walls were no longer cream, but a light shade of aqua.

It was the exact color I'd wanted, but that wasn't what had me in tears.

With the widest grin I'd ever seen, Sebastian stepped out of the way so I could see what he'd done. "What do you think?" he asked, beaming with excitement.

I walked over to the crib, running a hand over the smooth wood. "Did you make this?" It was perfect, the wood carvings so detailed and delicate.

He pulled me into his arms. "I did. I've been working on it for the past two months. When we find out if we're having a boy or girl, I'm going to carve their name right here," he said, pointing to the top wooden piece of the crib.

Biting my lip, I tried to keep from smiling. "It's amazing, I love it." I tried to block him from getting into my mind, but failed.

"What are you hiding from me? Is there something you know that I don't?"

I burst out laughing. "Okay, fine, I was going to tell you tonight, but I can't keep it a secret anymore. Seraphina was at my old house when I went to pick Amelie up to take her to Blake's. She kind of told me what we're having."

"Well?" he asked, eyes wide in joy. "What did she say?"

Stepping back, I placed my hands on my stomach. "We're having a girl," I announced happily.

Sebastian picked me up in his arms and twirled me around, hooting and hollering. With tears glistening in his eyes, he bent down and kissed my stomach before placing his lips on mine. "You have no idea how happy you just made me."

I felt the baby flutter inside me. Eyes wide, he glanced

down at my stomach, then back to me. He must have felt it too. "Was that her?"

I nodded. "She loves you too."

"What about you?" he asked, rubbing his thumb across my lips.

"Why don't you take me to the bedroom and I'll show you?"

Not wasting any time, he picked me up and carried me to our room. "You don't have to ask me twice."

THE END

Want more of the Royal Shifters Series? Next up, half-fae and half-shifter Laila is pulled in two different directions, one toward the mysterious fae prince and the other to the sexy second-in-command alpha of the Teton pack. Find out who she chooses in Rise of the Moon.

ABOUT THE AUTHOR

New York Times and USA Today bestselling author L. P. Dover is a southern belle living in North Carolina with her husband and two beautiful girls. Everything's sweeter in the South has always been her mantra and she lives by it, whether it's with her writing or in her everyday life. Maybe that's why she's seriously addicted to chocolate.

Dover has written countless novels in several different genres, including a children's book with her daughter. Her favorite to write is romantic suspense, but she's also found a passion in romantic comedy. She loves to make people laugh which is why you'll never see her without a smile on her face.

You can find L.P. Dover at www.lpdover.com
Email: authorlpdover@gmail.com

ALSO BY L.P. DOVER

In the Crossfire

**ARMED & DANGEROUS/CIRCLE OF JUSTICE
CROSSOVER SERIES**

Dangerous Game

Dangerous Betrayals

Book 3 - TBD

Book 4 – TBD

GLOVES OFF SERIES

A Fighter's Desire

Part One

A Fighter's Desire

Part Two

Tyler's Undoing

Ryley's Revenge

Winter Kiss: Ryley and Ash

Paxton's Promise

Camden's Redemption

Kyle's Return

SOCIETY X SERIES W/HEIDI MCLAUGHLIN

Dark Room

Viewing Room

Play Room

FOREVER FAE SERIES

Forever Fae

Betrayals of Spring

Summer of Frost

Reign of Ice

ROYAL SHIFTERS SERIES

Turn of the Moon

Resisting the Moon

Rise of the Moon

BREAKAWAY SERIES

Hard Stick

Blocked

Playmaker

Off the Ice

STANDALONE NOVELS

Easy Revenge

Love, Lies & Deception

Going for the Hole

Anonymous

Love, Again

Fairytale Confessions

THE DATING SERIES W/HEIDI MCLAUGHLIN

A Date for Midnight

A Date with an Admirer

A Date for Good Luck

A Date for the Hunt

A Date for the Derby

A Date to Play Fore

A Date with a Foodie

A Date for the Fair

A Date for the Regatta

A Date for the Masquerade

A Date with a Turkey

A Date with an Elf

CHRISTMAS NOVELS

It Must've Been the Mistletoe

Snowflake Lane Inn

Wrapped Up with You – December 2021

MOONLIGHT AND ALEENA SERIES
W/ANNA-GRACE DOVER

Moonlight and Aleena: A Tale of Two Friends

Printed in Great Britain
by Amazon